# Wild Fire

Wakara of Eagle Lodge

1

# Wild Fire

## LINDA I. SHANDS

Fleming H. Revell
A Division of Baker Book House Co
Grand Rapids, Michigan 49516

Published by Fleming H. Revell
a division of Baker Book House Company
P.O. Box 6287, Grand Rapids, MI 49516-6287

Printed in the United States of America

**Library of Congress Cataloging-in-Publication Data**

Shands, Linda I., 1944-
    Wild fire / Linda I. Shands.
       p.   cm. —(Wakara of Eagle Lodge ; 1)
    Summary: A year after her mother's death in a fire, fifteen-year-
old Wakara still struggles with grief, while she and her family try to
continue with life at their remote mountain lodge in the Oregon
wilderness.
    ISBN 0-8007-5746-7
    [1. Grief—Fiction. 2. Identity—Fiction. 3. Single-parent fami-
lies—Fiction. 4. Forest fires—Fiction. 5. Survival—Fiction. 6. Chris-
tian life—Fiction. 7. Oregon—Fiction.] I. Title.
PZ7.S52828 Wi 2001
[Fic]—dc21                            00-053360

For current information about all releases from Baker Book House, visit our
web site:
                http://www.bakerbooks.com

To

# Wakara Windbird Jackson

Thank you for sharing
your beautiful name

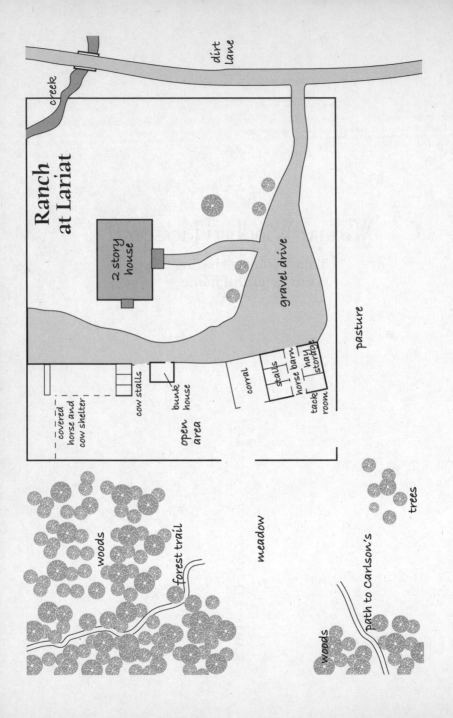

Ranch at Lariat

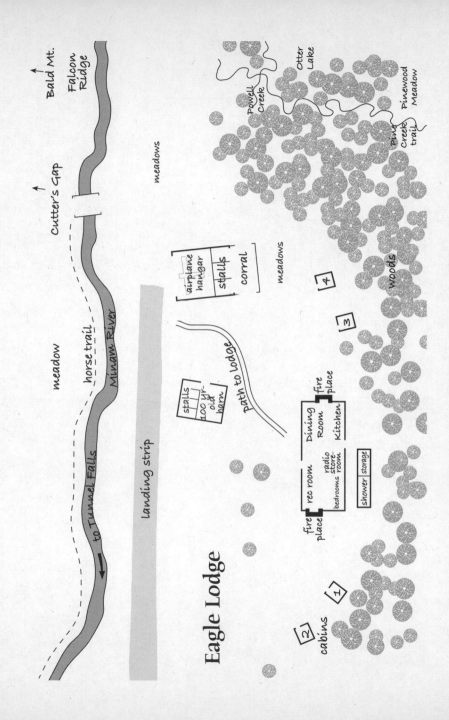

Eagle Lodge

Bald Mt.
Falcon Ridge

Cutter's Gap

meadows

to Tunnel Falls

horse trail

Minam River

meadow

Powell Creek

Otter Lake

Pine Creek trail

Pinewood Meadow

woods

airplane hangar

stalls

corral

meadows

4

3

Landing strip

stalls

100 yr old barn

Path to Lodge

fire place

Dining Room

Kitchen

rec room

radio store-room

bedrooms

fire place

shower

storage

1

2

cabins

# 1

FIFTEEN-YEAR-OLD WAKARA SHERIDAN could not remember having a nightmare since the start of second grade. Back then she had dreamed her new teacher was a witch who locked little children in closets and gobbled them alive after school.

Mom had heard her screams and rocked her back to sleep, whispering, "Everything will be all right." And of course it was. In fact, that teacher had turned out to be one of Wakara's favorites.

But this time it was different. The nightmares had started halfway through her sophomore year. Exactly six months, three weeks, and two days after Mom died. They were always terrifying and always the same.

*She and Mom were trapped in a raging forest fire. They were holding hands, running through the woods. The river was just on the other side of that gully. If they could cross it, somehow Kara knew they'd be safe. Suddenly Mom pulled away and started running in the opposite direction. Kara tried to call her back, but the flames were all around them and she couldn't breathe. She took one step forward, then she was falling. She tried to scream, but nothing came out.*

Kara awakened like she always did, soaked in sweat, her heart pounding, her mouth dry as ashes. It took several minutes for the fear to fade while she reminded herself that she was in her own room, at the house in Lariat, with Dad and Greg and Ryan just down the hall.

She swung her legs over the edge of the bed, closed her eyes, and sat with her head down until the shaking stopped. Mom couldn't comfort her now. The car crash and fire had taken care of that.

A muted light behind the window shade told her it was early morning. She pulled on some sweatpants and headed for the bathroom. She might as well get up; there was a lot to do today.

She hadn't told anyone about the dreams, not even her best friend, Tia. They'd think she was crazy. She wasn't even there when Mom was killed, let alone running through any flames.

By the time she had washed and dressed, she'd managed to put the nightmare out of her mind.

▲

*Wakara Windsong Sheridan.* Kara added a pigtail flourish to the *n* on her last name and tossed the sheet of paper toward the bed. Tia snatched it in midair, stuffed it into an envelope, then added it to the top of the pile.

"Nice catch." Kara stretched backward, arching her head until her thick, black braid touched the floor. Dressed in blue jeans and a white, long-sleeved T-shirt, she'd been sitting at her computer desk all morning typing envelope labels and requests for college catalogs.

"That's the last of them. I don't know why Dad insists I send for these now. I've got two years 'til college. Vet school is another millennium away."

10

Tia rolled her eyes and flopped over onto the pillow. "Don't act so martyry. At least you get a chance at college. You're a whole year ahead of me, and I'll be lucky to graduate."

Kara grinned. "No doubt. Anyone who says 'martyry' deserves to be stuck in high school for the rest of her life."

Tia stuck out her tongue. "Mom says I'm creative."

Kara turned away quickly, but not before her friend saw the pain in her eyes.

Tia scrambled off the bed. "Sorry. I'm such an idiot!"

Kara lifted the small silver frame from its place of honor on her dresser and studied the picture. "Don't worry about it," she said softly. "You have a right to talk about your mom. I just have to get used to being without mine."

She put the picture down and looked around the room. It was small but neat. She'd painted the walls herself—a soft, ivory color with just a hint of blue. Her older brother, Greg, had helped her revarnish the hardwood floor, and she'd found the perfect throw rug at a garage sale. The project had been fun, but if it was supposed to help her get over her mother's death, it hadn't worked.

She retrieved the stack of letters from the foot of the bed and set them on the desk. "I'll mail these later." She forced herself to sound cheerful. "Let's go for a ride."

Tia's face brightened. "Yeah, let's." Then she sobered again. "I can't believe you're leaving tomorrow. What am I gonna do all summer without you?"

Kara concentrated on lacing up her riding shoes. The two friends had planned to spend the summer at Eagle Lodge cleaning cabins and playing hostess to the guests. But Tia had gotten an F in History and had to retake the class in summer school.

*Your own fault,* Kara thought, but she didn't say it out loud.

She heard the rattle of a pickup on the gravel drive and followed Tia to the window.

11

Tia gasped. "Oh, wow. Who's that?"

Kara leaned around her friend's shoulder and peered down into the yard. "That's Colin. Dad hired him to work as wrangler at the lodge this summer."

"He's cute!"

Kara laughed at the look on Tia's face. She had thought the same thing when she'd met Colin a few days ago. His hair was the color of sun-dried wheat, and his light brown eyes were flecked with green.

She watched him climb out of the battered '87 Ford. Dusty brown boots, faded blue Wranglers, and a wilted black cowboy hat. A green plaid flannel shirt stretched tight across broad shoulders.

"Come on." She tugged on Tia's arm. "I'll introduce you to him."

Colin and Greg were on the porch, Greg lounging on the built-in bench while Colin leaned against the railing. Colin straightened and pulled off his hat when Kara stepped outside, letting the screen door slam behind her.

"Hi, guys, what's up?" Kara tried to hide her grin. She could guess at the expression on Tia's face without even looking at her. Tia had this thing about meeting new guys— a frantic combination of eagerness and awe. It never lasted long, though. Tia didn't date any more than she did.

Greg looked irritated at the interruption. Colin's smile caused his eyes to crinkle at the corners. The green flecks sparkled.

Kara quickly turned to Tia. "Tia, this is Colin Jones. Colin, this is my friend Tia Sanchez."

Colin nodded at her friend. Tia's eyes were a deep chocolate brown, and right now they were the size of Frisbees.

"Hi. I was just asking Greg about that paint." Colin pointed to where Tia's gelding, Patches, was tied at a post halfway between the driveway and the barn. "He belong to you?"

Tia nodded, still speechless, and Colin's gaze shifted back to Kara. "Nice horse. You ladies going riding? That meadow trail's still slick in places, but it's better than the one up Sutter Hill. Greg here nearly lost it up there this morning. Dakota managed it, but I think we need a week or two of sun before it's safe."

Greg's face turned red, and Kara urged Tia on down the steps.

"We'll be careful," she grinned. Colin ducked his head and settled his dilapidated hat back in its place.

Tia was untying Patches but still looking toward the porch. "He's gorgeous! And he's spending the summer at Eagle Lodge? You have all the luck."

Kara shrugged, "He's nice enough, but he's bossy. And," she added as she unhooked the barn gate, "he talks too much."

Tia sighed and led Patches into the barn. "I didn't notice."

Once in the barn, Kara forgot about Colin. She put a halter on her mare, Lily, and led her to the grooming mat. The pretty palomino nickered with excitement as Kara readied her for the ride.

Patches stood patiently at the end of his lead rope. His black and white coat still gleamed from this morning's brushing. Tia had ridden him from her place to Kara's, so he was already saddled. "Where's Ryan?" Tia asked as she looked around the empty yard.

Kara buckled the cinch strap under Lily's belly. "Don't panic. My little brother is at his friend Timmy's for the afternoon."

"Well, hurry up. If he comes home early, he'll want to go with us."

"Not a chance. I'm all set." She lifted her left foot into the stirrup, hopped three times on her right, then swung it over and settled into the saddle.

13

Tia giggled. "When are you gonna grow legs? I'll get the gate so you don't have to get off again."

Kara wrinkled her nose good-naturedly. She was used to being teased about her height, or rather, her lack of it. She hit the charts just under five foot one and hadn't grown an inch in over a year. "I may be short," she challenged, "but I can outride you any day."

Tia's eyes flashed. "You're on."

The girls kept their horses at a walk through a patch of evergreens and across a small stream. The winding trail ended at the edge of a field. Bare and muddy all winter, the meadow was now a wide expanse of lush, green grass and wildflowers.

"Race you," Tia yelled. She spurred her horse into a gallop.

Seconds later Kara was riding alongside, then past her. She loved the feel of the wind on her face, the horse's muscles leaping under her as they crossed the meadow with powerful strides.

She knew the tears would come now, but it was okay to cry. Her friends, her counselor, even Dad had said so. And it was safe to cry while riding Lily. Lily wouldn't look at her with pity or turn away embarrassed like some people did.

Kara couldn't blame them, though. What do you say to someone whose mom has died? "I'm sorry." "Give it time." "Trust God." None of those things helped.

When they were close to the tree line, she eased her mare into a canter, then into a slow trot. Tia rode up beside her, panting and laughing, patting her horse's neck. "Wow, that Lily can go. I don't see how you stay on her."

If she noticed Kara's tear-stained face, she didn't say anything. "Patches is in a lather. We'd better keep them at a walk on the way back."

Kara nodded. She'd miss Tia. Summer wouldn't be the same without her friend, but at least she'd have Lily.

# 2

THE HORSES HAD COOLED DOWN by the time they reached the barn. Kara noticed a patch of dark clouds to the west and hurriedly unsaddled Lily. "Looks like we might have a storm."

Tia led Patches toward a vacant stall. "Do you want me to stay? I've got an hour to kill before Pops gets home."

Kara wanted to hug her. "Thanks. I feel so stupid. I used to love storms."

Tia shrugged. "Don't worry about it. Stuff happens."

They gave each horse a flake of hay and ran for the house, ducking hail-sized splats of rain.

They had just shut the door when the room darkened. Tia hit the light switch as thunder cracked outside the window, rattling the shade. The lights flickered. Kara froze, then felt Tia's hands squeeze her shoulders. "It's okay. It'll be over soon."

Kara's laugh sounded more like a crow squawk. "If you weren't here, I'd probably be hiding under the bed." She shivered. If Mom were here, they'd be curled up by the fire reading mystery novels and counting the seconds between flashes.

Lightning streaked across the window, and another crack of thunder sounded directly overhead. Kara ducked and dove for the couch. Tia sat down next to her. "Give yourself a break. It hasn't even been a year."

Kara raised her head and saw the tears in Tia's eyes. "Oh, Tia, sometimes I miss Mom so much I wish I'd died too."

"Well I'm really glad you didn't. Then I'd have to hang out with Krista Stoner, and she's, like, so up all the time. I'd never get in a good cry."

Kara blinked, then burst out laughing.

The storm was over in less than half an hour. Tia helped her stamp envelopes, then they dug a suitcase and sports bag out of Kara's closet and began to pack her things.

Tia looked at her watch. "I gotta go." She snatched up the stack of envelopes. "I'll mail these for you in the morning."

Kara stuffed her green sweatshirt in the duffle bag and zipped it shut. "Thanks. You've been a big help already." She drew a deep breath. "Eagle Lodge, here I come. I wish . . ."

She didn't finish the sentence. Tia already felt bad enough about not going. Kara didn't want to make things worse. Instead, she wrapped Tia in a friendly hug. "Come on, I'll walk you to the barn."

Tia and Patches had just disappeared around the curve in the gravel road when Colin's truck skidded around the corner, kicking up rocks and flinging mud in all directions. He passed Kara, then came to a screeching halt a few yards down the drive.

The door hinges squealed as Colin jumped out and jogged back toward her. His eyes widened at her mud-speckled face and T-shirt. "Wakara, I'm sorry. I didn't see you. Are you okay?"

She wanted to yell at him. *No, I'm not!* Now she'd have to take a bath and do a load of laundry before she could get dinner on the table. And she still wasn't finished packing. She sighed. It was going to be a long night.

Colin was beginning to look worried, and she realized she hadn't answered him. "I'm fine." She managed a smile. "A little dirt never hurt anyone."

Colin's face relaxed. "I've been out at the south pasture checking the stock." He gestured toward the muddy truck. "They're all a little slow and overweight, but a few days up in the mountains and they'll toughen right up."

Kara knew the saddle horses they would use for trail rides at the lodge had been in the barn most of the winter and had feasted on rich pasture grass all spring. She didn't doubt that they were out of shape.

Before she could think of anything more to say, a horn honked at the end of the drive.

Colin touched his hat. "I'm glad you're okay. See you in a couple of days."

As he sprinted off to move his truck, Kara noticed the red-and-white sticker on the back bumper. LET GO, the first line read. Then underneath in bold letters, AND GET A GRIP ON GOD. She started to call out and ask him what it meant, but the truck was already moving down the road.

A dark blue Land Rover took its place in the drive. The passenger door flew open and a blond-haired, blue-eyed, six-year-old tornado launched himself at her.

"I'm home, Kara. What's for dinner?" Her little brother, Ryan, tugged her toward the house. "Come on. I gotta hurry and pack. We're leaving tomorrow. Whoa, you're sure dirty; wait 'til Dad sees. You're in big trouble!"

Kara laughed and untangled his hands from around her arm. "Don't worry about it. Did you thank Mrs. Crandall for the ride?" Ryan nodded. Kara waved, then turned back toward the house. She'd better get a move on. Dad

17

would be home any minute, and she hadn't even started the spaghetti.

She helped Ryan wash his hands and got him started buttering the French bread, then she grabbed a quick shower and changed into clean sweats. By the time Dad walked in the door, the aroma of spicy tomato sauce and warm garlic bread wafted through the house.

"Hi, Sugar Bear, how was your day?" He bent and kissed the top of her head.

"Fine." Kara winced at the dark circles around his eyes. He'd been working too hard. Like that was going to make him forget.

Since Mom died, Dad had been pouring all of his energy into running the ranch. He hardly ever sat and watched TV with them anymore, and she would see his light on late at night. "Doing book work," he said. But Kara suspected he spent a lot of time just staring into space. More than once she'd gone into his office to check on him, and he hadn't even known she was there.

Ryan burst into the room, his backpack slung over one shoulder. "Dad! I'm ready to go, see? There's even room for my videos."

While Dad tried to explain to Ryan why he couldn't take his videos of old John Wayne movies, Kara finished setting the table. Poor Ryan. He wasn't much of a reader yet, and there was no TV at the lodge. No electricity either, except when they ran the generator. Ryan polished off his spaghetti and reached for the last slice of bread. Kara snagged the basket. "Eat some salad, Ry. You've already had three pieces." She looked at Dad for support, but he was concentrating on the latest *Cattleman* magazine. She finally split the bread with Ryan and threw the last of his salad down the garbage disposal.

She had tried to talk Dad into letting her ride in to the wilderness lodge with her brother Greg and the rest of the herd, but he'd insisted she fly in tomorrow with him and Ryan.

"There's too much to do, Wakara," he'd said. "I need your help getting the cabins in shape. Besides, if you don't come, who'll watch Ryan? We have to work together on this."

He was right, but why did she always have to be the one responsible for Ryan? *Because there is no one else, that's why.*

She packed the last of her things and set her clothes out for morning. It was close to midnight, but she had a hard time falling asleep.

Last year, preparing for the trip to Eagle Lodge had been exciting. Mom had fixed their dinner, helped Ryan pack his clothes, and then read him a story. After he had settled down for the night, she had spent time in Kara's room talking about their plans.

Ten months ago all Kara had to worry about were her grades and which outfit she was going to wear. Now she had to take care of Ryan, do all Mom's chores, and do her schoolwork besides. It just wasn't fair.

*Quit whining, Wako. No one ever promised you that life would be fair.* She used the nickname Greg had pinned on her when Dad was out of hearing range. She hated it, but lately it seemed to fit her state of mind.

She had a lot of work to do, but at least she could scratch the schoolwork for now. Yeah, three months in some of the most beautiful wilderness in the world, and all she had to look forward to was cleaning toilets and scrubbing floors.

19

# 3

RYAN CHATTERED ALL THE WAY to the small airport on the outskirts of Lariat. Kara tried to concentrate on the scenery. To their left, the rugged Wallowa Mountains shot straight up into the silver morning mist. She knew their jagged peaks were still spiked with snow.

Behind that range of mountains was another, just as rugged. The Minam Valley was sandwiched in between.

The small, four-seater Cessna was already waiting on the tarmac. A brown-and-green logo of crossed antlers against a background of trees had been freshly painted on the front passenger door.

"Pretty neat, huh?"

Kara understood the pride in her father's voice. He had worked hard to buy that plane and fix up Eagle Lodge.

She walked over and gave him a hug. "It looks great, Dad."

She glanced back up at the mountains. "But are we going to get out of here?"

Her dad followed her gaze and gave her shoulders a squeeze. "It is pretty thick up there. We'll give it an hour, then decide."

She felt a surge of disappointment. If the cloud cover stayed, they might not get over the mountains today at all.

It wasn't the clouds at the top that would cause a problem. Dad could navigate the peaks by radar. But if the mist continued on down the other side, they wouldn't be able to follow the narrow flight path, or see well enough to land the plane.

"Let's go get coffee in the pilots' lounge."

Dad said it with a straight face, but Kara laughed. The pilots' lounge was a tiny, one-room office with a scarred desk, a sofa, and a coffeemaker. She poured two mugs of coffee and handed Ryan change for the Coke machine.

An hour later the mountain peaks were still obscured by clouds. "What do you say we pop on up and have a look? If it's too dense on the other side, we can turn around."

"All right!" Ryan raced toward the car and started to drag his duffle bag to the plane.

She grinned and followed. By the time they loaded their gear in the tail and climbed into the "sardine can," as Tia called the tiny plane, it was almost eleven o'clock.

The engine turned over. Kara's stomach fluttered as the airplane coasted toward the runway. Ryan was up front with Dad. She leaned forward and tugged on his seat belt.

"Hey!"

"Just checking, Ry."

She clutched the armrest as the plane picked up speed. A few seconds later they were in the air.

When the plane leveled off, she lifted her head from the seat back and watched the scenery below. Grassy fields and ploughed farmland. Small stands of fir trees. Houses and barns lay scattered below the foothills like playing pieces on a brown-and-green checkerboard.

She held her breath as Dad guided the plane into the clouds above the mountains. This part was always a little spooky, like flying through spun cotton. You couldn't see the mountains or the sky.

21

The plane bumped, then dropped. Kara's breath came out in a whoosh as they broke through into the sun.

"We're in!" Dad's shout was jubilant. "Hang on, we're going to make the turn."

One minute Kara was admiring the treetops, the next all she saw was the rugged canyon wall.

Ryan squealed and twisted in his seat. "Oh, Daddy, make it stop. I want to get out."

"Hang on, Tiger, we're almost there."

Kara shouted over the noise of the engine. "Look, Ry, there's the runway. Remember?"

Dad chuckled. "Forget it, Sugar Bear, his eyes are closed. It's okay, Ryan, we're about to land."

They bumped along the strip of hard-packed dirt that ran alongside the Minam River and coasted to a stop just a few feet from the hand-carved wooden sign announcing Eagle Lodge.

Dad unlatched Kara's door, then went to lift Ryan out of the plane.

Kara jumped to the ground and stood staring at the ruined corral. "Whoa! If the rest of the place looks like this, we'll be lucky to open by August."

She tossed her braid over her shoulder, stepped across the flattened wire that was once a fence, and stopped short at the water trough. It was clogged with mud and pine boughs. Next to it lay a large, gray block of what looked like fur-covered cement.

"This saltlick looks like the deer have used it for an antler rub."

"They probably did."

Kara turned at her father's chuckle. Instead of the despair she expected to see, his eyes sparkled with quiet laughter. He patted the back of her Levi jacket. "Don't worry, Sugar Bear, we'll have it back in shape in no time."

22

In spite of the winter damage, Kara loved this wilderness paradise. Her parents had bought Eagle Lodge a year ago last spring. Besides the main lodge, there were four log cabins, a spider-infested outhouse, an ancient barn, and what used to be a small corral.

"Didn't you say the guys are bringing in the stock tomorrow? What are we going to do with a dozen horses and no corral?"

Greg and Colin were to lead the horses, including Lily and Ryan's pony, Star, into the valley by way of a narrow switchback trail down from Pine Creek. It was a slow trip and could be dangerous, especially this time of year when parts of the trail would still be blocked by snow and fallen logs.

Kara smiled. She wondered what Colin would think of that trail. Greg had been up and down it several times, but she would bet Colin hadn't seen anything like it. It would have been fun to ride in with them.

Colin. He was seventeen, a year younger than Greg, and, she had to admit, much better looking than any of the boys at home. He did talk too much, but that was better than her brother's sullen silence.

She pushed aside her thoughts and followed her father's gaze. He motioned to the runway where the Cessna still waited to be taxied into the hangar. "We'll turn the horses out there. The pasture fences by the river look like they held up all right."

Kara studied her father's face. How could he be so calm?

They had been standing in almost this very spot the last time they saw Mom. It hadn't even been a year. Her eyes stung. She started to ask him if he remembered too, but his attention was fixed on a blur of activity down by the river.

"Ryan!" he shouted. "Get away from that water, now, and make yourself useful."

23

Her father headed back toward the runway. "You and Ryan drag those sacks of grain into the barn, while I tie down the plane. We're supposed to have high winds tonight."

Kara groaned but did as she was told. Grabbing the end of one fifty-pound sack, she muscled it around until she had enough of a grip to half drag, half carry it into the barn.

Telling Ryan to make himself useful was a joke! He was small for his age. All arms and legs, skin and fragile bones. And always getting into trouble. "An accident waiting to happen," their mother had said.

*The best way he can help is to stay out of the way.* But she didn't want to hurt his feelings, so she dragged six sacks into the barn and waited, tapping the toe of her boot on the muddy ground, while he pushed and pulled a bag of oats through the narrow door.

He came out sweating, eyes gleaming with pride. "We did it." The satisfaction in his voice made Kara smile. "We helped Dad a lot, didn't we, Kara?"

She brushed a hunk of shaggy blond hair off his forehead. "Yeah, Pest, we helped him a lot. Now, let's go see what the rest of the place looks like. I have a feeling we're going to be helping from now 'til September."

Ryan bolted away, giving Kara time to inhale a breath of mountain air. She remembered the first time they had put Eagle Lodge in order. Talk about work! She felt tired just thinking about it.

She and Greg and Mom had put in twelve-hour days, scrubbing walls, sanding furniture. Dad flew in on weekends to help with the heavier chores. By the end of August, they'd had the place almost habitable.

They'd be going home soon, and Mark, the charter pilot Dad had hired, took Mom back to Lariat to get the ranch house ready. Dad and Greg had stayed at the lodge with Kara and Ryan to finish sealing the inside cabin walls.

Thunderstorms had rocked the whole northeastern corner of the state that day. Mom must have been headed into town for supplies, on the curvy road from the ranch to Lariat, when lightning struck a tree. It had fallen in front of her car. The car had gone off the road, over a cliff, then exploded, setting the woods on fire.

Kara shuddered. Six months later she had started having nightmares, like the one she'd had the other night about being trapped in a raging fire.

She wiped her cheeks with the back of her hands. Crying just caused more grief for Dad. And Ryan. Ryan had it in his head that God would bring his mother back someday. "God just borrowed her for a while," he kept insisting. "He knows we need her here. He'll let her come home again soon."

He hadn't said that in a while, but it still made her angry. He was old enough to know better. He just didn't want to admit that Mom wasn't coming back. God hadn't bothered to save their mother when the accident happened. He certainly wasn't going to resurrect her now.

# 4

THE SKY HAD CLEARED to a deep, cobalt blue, and the air was getting warmer. Kara peeled off her jacket. Dad had already hauled the luggage up the hill in the small trailer attached to the tractor.

She tied the jacket around her waist and followed.

The main lodge was actually smaller than their ranch house in Lariat. She climbed the five steps to the wooden deck and ran her hand across the smoothly varnished log railing. They had restored the wood last summer, sealing it against the rain and snow. From what she could see, their hard work had paid off.

The screen door squeaked as she pushed it open and stepped into the entryway. Dad had told Greg not to oil it. "It doesn't hurt to know when someone's coming or going."

A musty smell of stale air and wood smoke made her sneeze. She stood still, allowing her eyes to adjust to the dim interior. The first thing they needed to do was open all the windows. She could hear Dad around back, already taking down the heavy shutters.

On her right was the recreation room. At the far end, a brown Naugahyde sofa and two padded wooden chairs clustered around a huge, rock fireplace. Books, puzzles, and games were stacked on the built-in shelves along one wall, and a pool table, covered with a plastic tarp, stood in the middle of the room.

Straight in front of her the stairway climbed to what had once been a bunkhouse. They had cleaned it up and turned it into a kind of master suite. Mom and Dad were supposed to live up there. Now Dad said the large bedroom and sitting room would be fine for the new cook, a woman named Anne.

"Why should she get the biggest room?" Kara had asked. Dad had mumbled something about not needing it now, and the look on his face made her want to cry. She decided not to push it.

Off the rec room, down a short hallway, were three small bedrooms and Dad's tiny office. He called it his hole in the wall. After moving in a desk and chair, there was hardly room to turn around, but he'd managed to squeeze in a small cot. The bedroom he was supposed to share with Ryan was right next door, but Kara doubted if he'd use it much.

When Greg stayed over, he'd share Colin's space across from Dad. Kara had chosen the small room at the end of the hall.

Instead of going to inspect her bedroom, Kara turned left into the dining area and wound her way around the oil-cloth-covered tables to the kitchen.

She stopped in the doorway and almost doubled over with the pain of memory. The floor was littered with newspaper, and half-empty packing cartons cluttered the counters. Open cupboard doors, scattered dishes, pots and pans—it all remained exactly as they'd left it when Sheriff Lassen brought the news. "I'm sorry, but she's gone. There was nothing we could do."

*Don't think about it!* Kara spun around and headed back to the deck. Their lunch was in one of the backpacks. "I'll deal with the kitchen later," she promised herself. Right now Dad and Ryan were probably starved.

She set out the lunch things at the picnic table. Bologna sandwiches, apples, carrot sticks, and individual cartons of juice. Cooking wouldn't take much imagination for the next couple of days. They still had to bring in supplies.

"Look, Dad. Awesome!" Ryan pointed to a herd of at least fifty elk grazing in a meadow across the river.

"Awesome is right. Let's hope they hang around 'til fall."

Kara winced. Dad and Greg had talked about guiding hunting trips from Eagle Lodge this fall instead of out of Lariat like they usually did. That meant Dad would be away for weeks at a time.

She knew the trips added to the family income. But she hated running the ranch house alone. Especially on top of school. And taking care of Ryan.

She decided to change the subject. Maybe Dad would forget about the whole thing.

"Come on, Ry. Help me clean up this mess, and we'll go inspect the cabins and the rest of the lodge."

He was as excited as she knew he'd be. "All right! My room first."

Dad retrieved his battered, brown fishing hat from the bench beside him and swung away from the table. "Ryan's right. Why don't you check out the lodge first? See what needs doing before tomorrow. Our bedrooms need to be cleaned and aired out. And don't forget Anne's."

Kara groaned. Her back hurt already. "What about the cabins? How soon do we need to have them done?"

"Not for a while. Give me a chance to check them out before you go in, okay?"

He glanced toward the gun rack and Kara understood. There'd been bear tracks down around the corral and barn. No telling what else the animals had gotten into.

Ryan hustled off to the room he was sharing with his father. Kara whispered, "Be careful, Dad."

Her father's eyes softened, and he pulled her over for a hug. "Don't worry, Sugar Bear. I'll be fine."

They cleaned the downstairs bedrooms first, then the one set aside for the cook Dad had hired. By dinnertime, Kara was so tired she was glad they had to settle for canned soup.

Ryan fell asleep right after dinner, and Kara turned her attention to her own room. She pushed the bed against one wall, made it up with her own bedspread and the pillow she'd brought from home, then stacked her books, T-shirts, jeans, and shorts on the shelves.

A wooden table under the window already held a flashlight, a lantern, and the room's single lamp. She added her mother's picture and stepped back to admire the results.

"Not bad," she sighed. "Not good either, but it'll have to do."

There was one more thing in the suitcase. Kara lifted it out and hung it carefully on a nail just inside the bedroom door. Besides the picture of her mother, it was her most cherished possession: a charcoal sketch her great-grandfather, Irish Sheridan, had made of his Nez Perce wife.

Wakara's resemblance to her namesake was uncanny, and for the hundredth time she studied the young bride's face: The broad forehead, high cheekbones, and small, straight nose were a reflection of her own.

She was proud of her heritage and she liked her given name, but when she was younger, her friends had started calling her Kara, and the nickname stuck.

From the drawing, you couldn't tell about the first Wakara's skin. Kara's was just a little darker than Greg's and Ryan's, like she always had a summer tan.

"You are so lucky," Tia had told her a million times. "You'll never have to worry about makeup."

Kara was glad. She would rather be out at the barn or riding Lily than fooling with makeup. Tia was always looking for the right foundation to cover up her zits.

The mirror Dad had given her for her birthday stood propped against the wall next to the window. Tomorrow she would hang it on the back of her bedroom door.

She bent and peered into the glass. It was her eyes that really set her apart. They were a brilliant green-blue. "The color of a stormy sea," her mother had said.

Still, they were different, too different to suit Kara. To make matters worse, they would often darken to a muddy gray when she was upset or angry.

"Ah, the curse o' the Irish," Dad often teased. "You have your great-grandfather's blood too, you know."

Kara stuck out her tongue at the mirror. Enough. Mom would say she was being vain. She grabbed a pair of cotton pajamas from the small wardrobe next to her bed, slid her feet into thick-soled thongs, and pulled on her jacket. June nights were still cold here in the mountains, and the shower shed was out behind the kitchen.

As she passed the room her father shared with Ryan, she knocked softly on the door. When there was no response, she peeked in. Ryan lay curled up on his cot, covered to the chin with a heavy wool blanket. His tangled hair, still damp from the shower, clung to the pillowcase. His face looked pale but peaceful, and she was careful not to shine the light in his eyes.

"Needs a haircut, doesn't he?"

Dad's hand on her shoulder was gentle, and she answered with a nod. "I'll try and talk him into it tomorrow," she whispered, "if I can get him to sit still for two minutes."

Her father grinned and rubbed a hand across his brow into his own head of thick, brown hair. "Do you suppose you could fit me in too? I meant to get over to the bar-

30

bershop before we came, but . . ." His shrug told her he'd forgotten.

He'd been forgetting a lot of things since Mom had died, like when it was time to get groceries, or take the cat to the vet, or send Aunt Peg a birthday card. Kara had just naturally taken over those chores, as well as the cooking and cleaning, and caring for Ryan.

If Mom were here, she would have cut their hair a month ago. Kara turned her head so Dad couldn't see the angry tears that had sprung into her eyes. When she looked up he was walking away.

"I'm going to lock up out front," he called over his shoulder. "You'd better get to bed; Colin and Greg will have the string of horses here by mid-morning, and Mark is flying the new cook in around noon. I need you to show her the ropes."

*Show her the ropes?* Kara groaned. They hadn't done anything in the kitchen yet except brew a pot of coffee. She'd have to spend the morning taking inventory and making lists, when what she really wanted to do was help Colin and Greg get the horses settled.

She hurried across the big, wood-paneled dining room and through the cluttered kitchen. The shower room was just a few feet from the back door.

She stepped under the lukewarm spray, and once again her thoughts turned to Colin. Until April, Colin had been a fishing guide in Alaska. *But he does seem to know a lot about horses.* He was outgoing and friendly. The guests would take to him right away.

And then there was the new cook Dad had hired. Who was she? Would she be friendly or bossy? All Kara knew was that her name was Anne Lightfoot and she came from the Indian reservation in Idaho.

The generator turned off just as Kara finished drying her hair. She pulled on the warm flannel shirt over her pajamas

31

and hurried across the narrow strip of dirt. She locked the back door and headed toward her room.

Moonlight flooded through the dining room windows, illuminating the front deck. A movement caught her eye, and she stepped closer to the window.

Dad stood with his back to her, his hands clutching the railing, his head bowed. Was he praying or crying? She hesitated. Should she go out there? She shook her head in answer to her own question. There was no way she could comfort him. No one could.

*When will it stop? When will the pain go away?* She wanted to shout and stomp her feet. Instead she hurried to her room, crawled between the cool sheets, and pulled the covers up over her head.

**5**

WHEN THE ALARM WENT OFF at 6:45, Kara groaned. It seemed like she had just closed her eyes. She stuffed her head underneath her pillow to block the light streaming through the uncurtained window.

*Get used to it, girl. When the guests start arriving, you'll be up at 5:00.* She forced herself to fling off the covers. "Yikes, it's cold!" She reached for the warmups from Aunt Peg. She'd almost left them at home—who needed a sweat suit in summer, right? *Right. It's still 40 degrees out there.*

Breakfast was Pop-Tarts, warmed over the fire Dad had lit in the huge fireplace, and lukewarm apple juice. Then Dad promised Ryan he could help with the corral if he'd sit still for a haircut later. After they left, Kara began taking inventory in the cluttered kitchen.

She picked up paper as she went, stuffing it in cardboard boxes and setting the trash out behind the supply shed. All the glassware, dishes, and pots and pans needed washing, but they should have enough. So far her list boiled down to food items, paper goods, and extra lightbulbs.

She looked at her watch. Mark was flying Anne in at noon. Colin and Greg should arrive with the horses shortly before that. If she hustled, maybe she could be down at the barn when they came in.

The day was warming. She changed into jeans and a seafoam green T-shirt. *Sneakers for now—riding shoes later,* she promised herself, then she settled on the deck to finish out her list of needed supplies.

Greg and Colin were late, but the charter flight out of Lariat was right on time. Kara tried to stem her curiosity, but as the small bush plane bumped along the landing strip, she tossed her pad and pencil to a log bench on the deck and followed Ryan down the hill.

Anne greeted them with a smile. "Wakara," she said softly, "Little Moon. We will be friends."

There wasn't a hint of doubt in her voice, and Kara nodded. Why had she called her Little Moon? Anne held her gaze for a few seconds more, then focused on Ryan, who was bobbing around behind Kara pointing his finger and making gun sounds.

"Pow, Pow. I gotcha, ya dirty scum."

Kara rolled her eyes. "Ryan, cut it out." She smiled an apology in Anne's direction and dragged Ryan in front of her. "Too many John Wayne movies."

Anne nodded. She laid a gentle hand on his shoulder and bent to look in his eyes. "You are Ryan, fast and brave."

Ryan would not leave her side after that. He dogged their footsteps all afternoon while Kara was trying to show the new cook around the kitchen and storage shed.

They were so busy, she forgot to listen for the horses. When Colin stuck his head through the door, she nearly jumped out of her skin.

"Hey, Wakara, what's up? I thought you'd be waiting at the barn with a pail of grain. That horse of yours is wild! Kept trying to push ahead. I think she knew you were at the end of the trail."

Kara grinned. "I'm sure she remembered that trail. It was her favorite last summer."

She introduced him to Anne, then looked around the kitchen. "Sorry, I can't get away right now. Give Lily a treat for me, will you? I'll be down to brush her later."

"No problem."

He turned to Ryan. "Where ya been, kid?" He said with an exaggerated drawl. "I been lookin' all over for ya. What are ya doing in the kitchen with a bunch of women when ya could be outside helping me break in this new rope?"

Ryan frowned and looked up at Anne. Kara knew he was torn between his fascination with the new cook and his desire to be with Colin. She was just about to order him out, when Anne smiled and nodded toward the door.

"You will go," she said. "A stiff rope must be bent to be useful."

The boy's eyes brightened. He hitched up his jeans and swaggered after Colin. More John Wayne. Kara had to bite her lip to keep from laughing.

"A boy of six needs the company of men as much as he needs a mother," Anne murmured as she bent to inspect the oven in the butane gas stove. "Not so much, a girl just turned fifteen."

Kara felt her face flaming and realized she had been staring after Colin.

She quickly changed the subject. "That thing must be at least fifty years old, but it works, and you don't have to rely on electricity. Dad doesn't like to run the generator much during the day. He said he'd fill the butane tank this afternoon."

Anne smiled, reached for the cleanser and a brush, and began scrubbing.

For a few minutes Kara stood and watched, thinking about what she'd write to Tia: *Dad said she was in her forties.*

*She looks a lot younger to me. A little on the chunky side, and she's even shorter than I am! Her hair's mostly gray, but she wears it loose down her back with narrow braids on the sides. I wonder if mine would look good like that.*

Kara silently admired Anne's outfit—a purple shirt tucked into black stretch jeans. Her clothes had a crisp, just-ironed look.

She looked down at her own ratty tennis shoes, faded jeans, and dirt-smudged T-shirt. When she raised her head Anne was watching her.

"A white fringed blouse and short denim skirt, I think."

Kara noticed the stove was now free of grease. Anne had cleaned the entire thing while she just stood there. *Way to go, Wako.* Her cheeks felt hot. "I'm sorry. What did you say?"

"For the dance on Saturday," Anne replied. "The hostess must look her best."

"The dance . . . ?" Of course. The first guests would arrive Friday, and Dad had scheduled entertainment for Saturday night. Colin was expected to play his guitar and run the portable CD player. She was supposed to lead the line dancing. The thought of standing up in front of all those people made her want to throw up.

Anne's hand settled softly on her shoulder. "You will do fine."

She said it in such a positive tone, Kara almost believed her.

"I will settle my room now. Your horse has waited long enough, I think."

Kara didn't wait for a second invitation. She grabbed her boots and sprinted toward the barn.

Lily's nicker was muffled by a mouthful of hay. The feeder was full. So was the five-gallon water bucket. Someone had spread straw over the hard-packed dirt inside the stall.

She grabbed a brush from the tack box and slid open the stall door. Ryan skidded to a halt beside her. "Colin made

36

Star a bed too. And one for Dakota. The others have to sleep outside."

Lily started and Kara spoke softly, "Easy, girl." She turned to Ryan. "Slow down. You know you're not supposed to run in here." He hung his head and she relented. "Don't worry about the other horses; they like to be outside, remember?"

She heard Colin before she saw him. "Ouch. That's the third time today I've banged my head. We've got to get more light in here."

The huge wooden barn was at least a hundred years old. Solid log beams supported the hayloft, but the wide loading doors weren't quite as sturdy, and Dad had nailed them shut last summer. Now they stored hay and grain on a platform down below and used the small side door as an entrance. Not great for the horses, but once inside, the stall aisle was roomy, with a line of saddling stations on one side and rows of saddles and tack on the other.

The housing stalls where Lily, Star, and Colin's buckskin, Dakota, stayed were at the far end of the aisle.

"I got a light." Ryan took off in the direction of the voice. Colin had just come around the corner when Kara saw a flash and smelled sulphur.

Her skin tingled in a rush of fear, then anger. She was halfway down the aisle before she saw the match was out. Colin had a grip on Ryan's shoulder. When he saw Kara coming, he stretched out his arm as if to keep her away. "It's okay, Wakara. I've got the matches. Nothing happened."

"That's not the point!" She could hear the fire in her own voice. *Cool it. Yelling will just make it worse.*

Ryan was already sniffling as Colin handed the book of matches to Kara.

"Where did you get these?" Her voice was calm, but she couldn't keep out the edge of anger. *How would Mom have handled this?*

37

Ryan's voice was strained. "From the drawer in the kitchen. I'm putting together a survival kit. You got to have matches in a survival kit."

Colin's mouth twitched, and Kara flashed him a warning with her eyes. "In the kit, Ryan Sheridan, not in your pocket. You could have burned down the barn. You know better than to play with matches. Go get washed up for dinner."

Real tears flowed down his cheeks. "But I gotta brush Star. Colin said I could."

Kara took a deep breath. *Just who's in charge here anyway?*

Colin spoke up. "Better mind your sister. I'll brush Star tonight."

Ryan started to argue, then hunched his shoulders and hurried out of the barn.

Kara stuffed the matches in her pocket, spun around, and headed back to Lily's stall. She bent to pick up the grooming brush. When she straightened she felt Colin's hand on her arm.

"You okay?"

Kara forced herself to relax. "Sure, I'm fine. He just could have burned us out is all. What makes me mad is he knows better."

Colin grinned. "I remember when I was six . . ." He squeezed her arm. "Don't worry, you'll get through it."

*Easy for you to say.* Kara felt an odd mixture of frustration and gratitude over his concern. She moved away, ducked under the stall guard, and began to run the brush over Lily's neck and back. The mare turned her head and nuzzled Kara's shoulder. Kara buried her face in the sweet-smelling mane. "Oh, Lily, what would I do without you? You're the only one who understands."

# 6

THE NEXT MORNING KARA WALKED with Dad down the hill to the hangar where they kept the Cessna. She waved at Greg and Colin who were setting the last of the poles on the new corral. Colin waved back, but Greg acted like he didn't see her.

*What's wrong with him?* He'd been like that since after the funeral, and nothing anyone said or did seemed to make a difference. He did his work and was civil when he had to be, but she wondered if she'd ever get her older brother back.

She handed Dad a thick envelope. "Would you take this letter to Tia for me?"

"Sure, Sugar Bear." He kissed the top of her head. "I have to go by the house. Greg said they delivered the new radio, but he couldn't bring it in on horseback."

She watched him back the Cessna out of the hangar and taxi across the bumpy dirt to the harder surface of the runway. She shuddered as she watched the plane leave the ground, bank to the right, and disappear over the top of the ridge.

What would she do if he didn't come back? She didn't want to think about it. She turned away and nearly collided with Ryan.

"What are you doing here? You're supposed to be helping Anne."

Ryan frowned. "I wanted to say good-bye to Daddy." His eyes darkened, and he slid his hand into hers. "He's coming back, isn't he, Kara?"

She swallowed the lump in her throat and kept her voice light. "Of course he is, silly. He'll be back before you know it. Tell you what. Let's stop by the barn and take Star and Lily some peppermint."

"All right!" Ryan dropped her hand and raced toward the barn.

"Don't you dare go into that stall until I get there," she yelled, but he had already disappeared through the narrow door.

Kara stopped at the tack box to pick out a grooming brush. By the time she caught up with him, Ryan had Star's halter almost on, but the straps were twisted. The little gelding was tossing his head up and down.

"One of these days you're going to get hurt because you won't listen."

"I did too listen. I'm not in the stall."

She shook her head. It was true. He had opened only the top doors and was perched on the railing trying to wrestle Star into the halter and keep his balance at the same time. He'd be better off inside the stall. She was about to lift him down and retrieve the tangled halter when a figure stepped out of the shadows.

"Hey, kid, you gotta grow some to be a bronc rider." Colin steadied the tottering boy with one hand and gentled Star with the other.

Kara watched him help Ryan with the halter, his large hands guiding the boy's smaller ones. *No wonder Ryan likes him,* she thought. *Colin has a lot more patience than I do.*

"Need help with Lily?"

Even in the murky light, Kara could see the grin in Colin's eyes. She hoped he couldn't see her blush. "No thanks," she said casually, "I'll manage."

They groomed the horses, gave them each a peppermint treat, and turned them out to pasture.

Kara looked at her watch. "Oh no, it's almost eleven and I promised I'd help Anne finish cleaning the kitchen." She expected Ryan to howl about leaving the horses, but Colin intervened again.

"I'd be much obliged, Miz Sheridan, if Ryan could stay and help me mend the fence." He lowered his eyes, twisted his hat in his hands, and pasted on a goofy grin.

Kara didn't know if she wanted to thank him or sock him in the jaw. *Miz Sheridan. Right.* Sometimes he acted even younger than Ryan.

"Just see that he gets back to the lodge in time for lunch."
*Great. Now I sound like Mom.*

All she wanted was to escape before she made a bigger fool out of herself, but she forced herself to walk instead of run. Why did Colin make her act so weird? She'd never been this uptight around a guy before.

By late afternoon, the kitchen was spotless, the dining tables were set, and wood smoke trailed from the chimney. The musty smell had been replaced with the aroma of thick beef stew and fresh-brewed coffee.

Kara saw the pleasure in her father's eyes when he entered the room, both arms loaded with supplies.

"Whooee," he said, and whistled. "This place has never looked so good."

She felt a prickle of irritation. Mom had done a pretty good job of keeping things clean. She'd been a great cook too.

Greg and Colin followed him through the door carrying a large cardboard box. "This thing's heavy," Greg growled. "Where do you want it?"

"The radio." Dad answered Kara's unspoken question. "Put it in the storeroom off the kitchen for now. We'll get it set up tonight."

Kara rushed to hold the door while her brother and Colin lowered the heavy instrument to the floor.

Colin pulled a wrinkled bandanna from his back pocket and wiped the sweat off his face. "Whew, that thing better work. I'd sure hate to have to haul it back."

While they helped unload supplies, Anne poured cups of steaming coffee and handed them around. Dad disappeared again, then came back with a stack of boxes.

He cleared his throat and handed them to Kara. "Anne said you needed these." He looked uncomfortable. "I hope they fit."

Kara swallowed hard and opened the boxes. Along with a silky white blouse and light blue denim skirt were a pair of soft, white doeskin boots with rounded toes and decorative fringe along the sides.

"Dad! They're gorgeous. It's exactly what I would have chosen. How did you know?"

He laughed. "Thank Anne. She described what she thought you'd like and wrote down the sizes."

"But how could she know?" She looked into the kitchen. The guys were still unloading groceries, but the cook was nowhere in sight.

Kara didn't waste any more time thinking about it. "I want to try these on."

She put her arms around her father's neck and hugged him hard. "Thanks, Dad," she whispered. "Be right back."

Everything fit. Including the boots. They slid smoothly over her calves and felt soft as velvet against her skin. How could Anne have known? Mom would have known. *But she's not Mom.*

Kara took one more turn in front of the mirror. Her mother would have called the outfit stunning. It was perfect, and Kara decided to wait until Saturday night to show it off to the family. And Colin. She grinned at her reflection, then slipped out of the new skirt back into her jeans.

When she returned to the dining room, Anne was putting the food on the table, and Kara hurried to help her. It was on the tip of her tongue to thank the older woman for cluing Dad about the clothes, when Anne said, "The men are hungry; we will eat now."

"Sit here, Sugar Bear." Dad patted the seat next to his. "Anne can sit next to Ryan tonight. I thought you could use a break."

Kara glared at him. How could he use that stupid nickname in front of Colin? And why the change in seating arrangements? She always sat by Ryan.

She tried to catch her father's eye, but he had already bowed his head to say the blessing. She quickly clutched the hand he was holding out to her and shivered when she felt Colin grip hers on the other side.

"Father," Dad prayed, "we thank you for the food you have provided and for the hands that have prepared it. Thank you, too, for Anne, and for the ways she has already been a blessing to this family. Amen."

*A blessing to this family?* Dad's words made Kara steam. Sure, it was great to have Anne's help around the place, but she was just the cook. Was Dad going to let her run things? Was she trying to take Mom's place?

Colin's hand brushed hers as he passed the red potatoes, and she nearly dropped the bowl. *Get a grip, girl,* she told herself. *Colin's just another guy, and Anne's just a cook, and you are acting like a first-class idiot.*

43

She looked around the table to see if anyone had noticed. The men were busy eating. Ryan was sitting on his knees, intent on stabbing one more piece of potato onto his already full fork. But Anne met her gaze with gentle eyes and an understanding smile.

# 7

AFTER DINNER THE MEN DISAPPEARED into the storeroom to fiddle with the radio. Ryan tumbled out of his chair and raced after them. "Hey, wait for me, you guys. I get to help."

Kara helped Anne clear the table, then stared as the older woman ran dishwater into the sink.

"No sense running the dishwasher for so few dishes."

Kara groaned and grabbed a dish towel. Anne was right. Running the generator was expensive, and Dad had asked them to conserve energy whenever they could. She had wanted to wash her hair, but at this rate she wouldn't be out of the kitchen until after eight, and the generator would be shut down.

"The men will need the lights later tonight, I think." Anne interrupted her thoughts. "It will take them a while to set up the radio."

*And,* Kara thought, *I can do my hair.* She waited for Anne to say it. When the words didn't come, she laughed silently at herself. *You're paranoid, Wako. She may be smart, but she definitely can't read your mind!*

"If you're from the reservation in Idaho, you must be Nez Perce. Is that how you know my name means little moon?"

Kara couldn't believe she'd said the words out loud, but the woman just smiled and handed her the last plate.

"Wakara is not a Nez Perce name."

Kara nearly dropped the plate. What was she talking about? Of course Wakara was a Nez Perce name. Her great-grandmother was Nez Perce. Or was she? There had been some confusion about that.

"Wakara is a Yana name."

Kara felt a stab of irritation. "Yana? I've never heard of them." She dried the plate and set it on the open shelf above the sink.

When she turned back, Anne was watching her, a thoughtful smile on her face.

"Would you like to talk, Wakara?"

Kara hesitated. What she really wanted was a few minutes to herself. Anne had to be wrong but she was curious about what the woman had to say.

Anne poured hot water from the kettle on the stove into two mugs and added packets of cocoa mix. When the hot chocolate was ready, she led the way into the dining room and cleared a place at one of the smaller tables.

Kara blew on the hot liquid and had taken three sips before Anne began.

"What do you know of your great-grandmother's people?"

The question startled Kara. She had thought Anne would explain. "Some," she said slowly.

Anne nodded encouragement, so Kara told her what she knew.

"In 1917, my great-grandfather, Harley 'Irish' Sheridan, found this Indian woman and her baby in the woods. The woman had been shot. Before she died, she pushed the baby into his arms and whispered, 'Wakara.'

"He took the baby to the closest town. No one knew anything about the woman, but they decided she and the baby

46

must be from a band of Nez Perce still living on a nearby reservation.

"For some reason my great-grandfather didn't want to take the baby there, so he asked a missionary couple if they would keep her. Anyway, he told them the baby's name was Wakara and left her with them. When Wakara turned fifteen, he went back for her. He married her and took her to Portland.

"When Irish died, he left a drawing. A charcoal sketch of Wakara as a bride. Would you like to see it?"

When Anne nodded, Kara hurried to her room. Why was she so excited about this? But she knew the answer. She loved the story, and no one but Tia had ever been interested before.

She walked back to the table and slid the framed drawing in front of Anne. "There was a letter too, explaining about Wakara's background.

"I was the first girl in three generations. Dad says my Grandpa Sheridan came to the hospital when I was born, took one look, and said, 'Her name is Wakara.' He gave my parents the letter and the picture of his mother. They hung it in the nursery, and I've had it ever since."

Anne smiled. "Ah, it is right that your grandfather named you. She is beautiful, and I think you are very much alike."

Kara flushed. "Grandpa Sheridan named my dad Harley after his father, so I guess my folks thought it was fine for him to name me after his mother."

Kara sighed and picked up the picture. "The story's so romantic, but sad too. My great-grandmother died before she turned twenty-one. Grandpa Sheridan was raised by some cousins."

When Kara had finished, the woman touched her hand. "My father wrote a book about the Yana people."

"So, that's how you knew about the name?"

47

Anne nodded, picked up both mugs, and headed toward the kitchen. "The guests come tomorrow. We must get some sleep," she said.

"But . . ." Kara started to call her back. What if Anne was right? What if her great-grandmother hadn't been Nez Perce like they'd thought all along, but had belonged to these Yana people instead?

*Well, yeah,* she reasoned, *what if? That doesn't change a thing. Everything else is true.* But it was an eerie feeling to grow up thinking you were part of one nationality and then find out you were really something else.

Kara looked at her watch. Nine o'clock. The men were still bent over the radio, and Ryan had fallen asleep on the floor. What would they think about it? She shook her head. It wouldn't bother them a bit. Dad might be surprised, but neither he nor Greg nor Ryan had the slightest resemblance to the first Wakara.

Anne was already halfway up the narrow stairs to her room by the time Kara realized she had said "Good night."

Kara scooped up Ryan, tucked him into his own bed, and raced for the shower.

When she had turned off her lantern and crawled into bed, she tried to pray, but the things Anne had said kept crowding into her mind. Who was the first Wakara? It shouldn't make that much difference, but it did. If her great-grandmother was not Nez Perce, but a member of this Yana tribe, then so was she!

She had to find out. She had done most of the talking this time. Next time it was Anne's turn. She rolled over and tucked her hand under the pillow, pulling her knees to her chest in that comfortable position that always put her to sleep. She wanted to find out more about Anne's background too. There had to be a way to get her to talk about herself.

# 8

KARA'S EYES SNAPPED OPEN. Had that noise been in a dream? The room was dark as midnight except for a small patch of gray where the window was. She reached for the flashlight on the floor next to her bed, then lay still trying to listen over the pounding of her heart.

*Crash!*

There it came again. Then a high-pitched whinny that sounded almost like a human scream.

The horses!

She scrambled out from under the tangled blankets. The heavy flashlight hit the floor and rolled out of reach. She groped for her clothes in the darkness and yanked them on.

In the hallway, someone lit a lantern. She could see Greg tugging on his boots. Colin had the shotgun, and Dad was holding the .45.

Ryan tugged at her sleeve. "Kara, the horses. Something's wrong with Star. Come on, let's go."

She almost pushed him away, but the fear in his voice stopped her. She bent down and pried his fingers gently from her arm. "Not this time, Ry." She moved him carefully backward into Anne's waiting arms.

In the lantern light, the cook's face looked composed. *Unshakable.* The single word flipped through Kara's mind as the woman wrapped her arms firmly around Ryan's shoulders. Ryan struggled silently against her hold until she bent and whispered something in his ear.

Kara turned and raced out the door after the men.

Rifle shots echoed up the hillside, and Kara froze as a huge dark animal ran from the barn. It lumbered across the meadow and through the empty corral, then disappeared into the woods.

She bolted down the hill and ducked through the gaping hole where the barn door used to be. She stood still to let her eyes adjust to the darkness.

"Let's get some light in here." Dad's voice came from the direction of the stalls.

"I'll fire up the generator." Greg pushed past her, and she had to grab his arm to get his attention.

"What's happening?"

"Bear. After the grain."

Kara followed his pointing finger and could just make out several ripped-open grain sacks, the flakes of oats and corn scattered all over the ground.

She picked her way through the slippery grain, splintered wood, and bits of iron from the shattered door frame. When she got to the grooming area, Colin was already leading Lily out of her stall.

She heard rustling close by, then Dad's soft voice murmuring to Star. "Easy, boy, easy. It's okay now. You're just fine."

Lily nickered softly as Kara approached. Colin stepped around and handed her the halter rope. "As far as I can tell, she's okay. I found a small cut on her rump. She must have caught a splinter while she was dancing around."

Kara realized she'd been holding her breath, not knowing what she'd find. She let it out in a whoosh, then hugged the shaking mare.

"Can you take her?" Colin asked. "I've got to get out there and see about the other horses."

Kara heard the generator roar to life. As the overhead lights flashed on, she remembered the empty corral. Some of the horses had been penned there for the night.

"Be careful, Colin. That bear may still be around."

Colin smiled and brushed a strand of hair from her cheek. "Don't you worry, little lady," he drawled in his best John Wayne, "that ol' bear is clear to Mexico by now." He grinned, then turned and headed back through the broken door.

She felt her face burn. Why did Colin always have to act like a comedian?

Lily's ears pricked up, and Kara realized Dad was standing next to her.

"Need some help?"

She hoped her face was back to normal. "No. Thanks, Dad. I'm going to be a vet, remember? I can take care of it. Is Star all right?"

"Star's fine. Lily doesn't look too bad either. The first aid supplies are in that locker." He nodded to a wooden chest wedged between the tack room and the stalls.

"When you're done here, have Anne put the coffee on. Those horses that were in the corral could be scattered from here to Rock Springs." He sighed. "It's going to be a long night."

She nodded, then went to get some salve for Lily's wound. She tried to concentrate on what she was doing, but her mind kept going back to Colin.

He was seventeen, closer to Greg's age than hers. Besides, he could be a real goof sometimes with that phony accent and comedy routine. He talked too much, and flirted with every girl he met.

"He could charm the scales off a rattlesnake," Greg had said once. But she was the boss's daughter. Colin had to think of her as just a friend. *That's what he is, Wakara Sheridan. Colin Jones is just a friend.*

She turned her attention back to Lily, examining her sides and back, feeling her legs, looking for breaks or scrapes. Colin was right; except for the cut on her rump, the mare was sound.

Kara talked softly to the horse, using singsong sounds to calm her as she cleaned the wound with Betadine. Then she slipped on a rubber glove and coated the gash with ointment.

"There, that should do it. See?" She held out the jar of ointment. Lily sniffed it, giving her approval. "Leave it alone now, and it will heal in a day or two."

She led Lily back to her stall, took off the halter, and shut the door. In the next stall, Dakota thumped the floor with his foot. "What's the matter, boy? You jealous? I know Colin already checked you out."

She decided to check him anyway. Sure enough there was a rock embedded in his back foot. She picked it out, gave the big animal a rub on the neck, then went in to examine Star. The pony was standing like a statue, one back foot cocked, head drooping, eyes half closed.

Kara chuckled. "You don't let anything bother you for long, do you, old boy?" Dad had already looked him over. She backed off and let him sleep.

After giving Lily and Dakota an apple treat, she stored away the first aid kit, picked up the lantern her dad had left, and headed back to the house.

Smoke billowed from the chimney, and she could smell the coffee halfway to the lodge. As usual Anne was way ahead of her.

A sleepy-eyed Ryan met her at the door. "Is Star okay? Did Daddy shoot a cougar?"

She laughed and pulled him in for a hug. "Star is fine. It was a bear, not a cougar, and it ran away."

Anne's eyes questioned her over Ryan's shoulder.

"It was after the grain," Kara assured her, "but the other horses broke out of the corral, and the guys have to round them up."

Ryan pushed back and grinned up at her. "We knew they'd be okay 'cause we asked God to take care of them." His face grew sober. "I couldn't come to the barn because I had the most important job of all."

"Oh?" Kara wiggled her eyebrows. "And just what was the most important job of all?"

The little boy laughed, "To pray, silly. Anne and I prayed for the horses, and Dad and Greg, and Colin and you."

Kara glanced at Anne. Why should she be surprised? That's just what Mom would have done.

The cook returned her puzzled gaze with a smile. "A boy should be asleep at 3 A.M."

Ryan let Kara lead him back to bed. As she tucked the covers up under his chin, she heard him mumble, "Please don't let the bear come back."

"Don't worry, Ry." She remembered Colin's words and smiled. "That ol' bear is clear to Mexico by now."

Ryan giggled, then frowned. "You sound like Colin. Anyway, I wasn't talking to you."

"Oh." Kara blinked. "Then who were you talking to?" If she didn't get some sleep she'd be useless tomorrow.

Ryan looked surprised. "God, silly." He smiled and closed his eyes.

**9**

KARA YAWNED AS SHE HUNG fresh towels in cabin four and checked the pile of kindling next to the cast-iron stove.

She blinked as she stepped out the door into the bright morning sun. Finally. She was done with the cabins. Crossing the wide expanse of weedy grass, she made her way toward the main lodge.

Dad and Greg were down at the barn cleaning up scraps of wood and trying to replace the door. In the distance, she could just make out Colin leading a group of horses into the repaired corral. The horses had to be exhausted.

To her right, beyond a lodgepole fence, the land sloped gently for half a mile then plunged over the banks into the Minam River. The valley stretched on for miles, separating the swift-flowing water from the Blue Mountains to the north.

Snow still clung to the highest peaks, and Kara's breath puffed white in the cool morning air. She stuffed her hands in her pockets and stood very still. A moment later three yearling deer stepped cautiously from the thick stand of trees on her left. They crept into the meadow and began to feed on the tall grass.

The screen door slammed and Ryan charged onto the deck. "Wow! Kara, look at the deer!" He pointed excitedly as the three whitetails disappeared into the woods.

Kara shook her head. "Way to go, Peanut Brain. You scared them away."

"They'll be back. They always come back." He flashed a sheepish grin, then grabbed her hand. "Come on, Anne's making pancakes for breakfast."

She let him lead her into the lodge. He could be a total pain, but she couldn't stay mad at him for long.

Ryan bolted into the kitchen, but Kara stopped to re-check the guest register her father had left sitting open on one of the tables.

A couple from Arizona, a family of four, and three single men.

Kara shut the book. Maybe none of them would be interested in line dancing and she could just practice some new two-step turns with Colin.

"You are not dreaming of clean towels, I think."

She jumped, then returned Anne's teasing smile. "No," she admitted, "but the cabins are done. There's plenty of kindling, and I replaced the wicks in all the lanterns."

The cook nodded. "You worked hard. The guests will be comfortable."

The men banged into the room, stomping their boots on the entry mat, and tossed their hats and jackets onto the rack next to the door.

"Did ya catch the bear?" Ryan hollered over the din.

"Not this time, Tiger." Dad ruffled his hair, then turned to Anne. "Let's eat. I'm starved."

Kara followed them to the table and grabbed a chair on the other side of Ryan. Colin sat across the table next to Dad.

After grace, Dad poured syrup over a stack of pancakes and turned to Colin. "I know you want to track that bear, but we've got guests coming this afternoon, and we need to be sure everything here is under control first."

He sipped his coffee, then continued, "The Wilson kids are eight and ten. Neither one of them have ridden before."

Colin nodded and helped himself to six slices of bacon. "I figured that. I thought we'd put the boy on Star and the girl on that older mare. If we line her up in the middle of the string, she'll pretty much go along with the rest. And Star couldn't run off if you lit a fire under him."

Everyone laughed but Ryan. "Hey. Star's my horse."

Kara grabbed his juice glass before he could knock it over. "We talked about that, Ry, remember? Star is yours to ride this summer, but you have to share him with the guests."

Ryan frowned. "Then why don't you have to share Lily?"

She wanted to yank his ear. "Lily's too spirited; you know that. None of the guests could handle her."

"So? They can too. Kara has to share, Dad. Tell her."

Dad set his coffee cup on the table and looked from Kara to Ryan. "Sorry, Tiger, your sister's right. Lily needs an experienced rider, and we need Star for the younger kids. You'll have plenty of time to ride."

"Not fair!" Ryan howled and tried to push away from the table. The chair stuck, but his fork and plate went flying.

Kara grabbed his arm. "Ryan!"

"That's enough, young man." Dad's voice stayed level, but she could hear the steel in his tone.

Anne leaned over and retrieved Ryan's plate from the floor. "Kara will share Lily," she said quietly.

Ryan stopped struggling. Kara loosened her hold on his arm and turned with everyone else at the table to stare at Anne.

"With me," Anne continued calmly. "If we are to have fresh trout each Sunday night, I will need Lily to carry me to Otter Lake."

Her eyes questioned Kara over Ryan's head, but Kara turned her head away. Her temper flared. *How could she?* Anne hadn't even asked to borrow Lily. Wasn't it enough that she had taken Mom's place at the lodge? She'd taken over Ryan too. She was so good at everything. Now she wanted Lily.

Kara nearly bolted from the table. Everyone was probably staring, and she was sure to be bawling any minute. But when she lifted her head, she saw the others were bent over their plates, shoveling food. And Dad was watching Anne.

The older woman handed the plate and fork to Ryan. "The broom and dustpan are behind the kitchen door," she said.

To Kara's surprise, he obeyed without a word.

Dad said something to Colin, who nodded and shoveled in another mouthful of eggs. Anne didn't look her way, and Kara pretended to be interested in the men's conversation.

"Anything else we need to solve right now?" Dad was saying.

Greg shrugged. "Not on my end. Hot Shot here has the horses lined up. I'm out of here tomorrow morning."

Kara winced at her brother's sullen tone. She wished he wouldn't talk to Dad like that, or be so rude to Colin. If it had been anyone else Dad wouldn't stand for it, but after Mom's death he'd put up with a lot from Greg and his lousy attitude.

*What about your own attitude?* Kara ignored her conscience and tried to tune back in to her dad's voice.

"I appreciate your willingness to take care of things at the ranch. Be sure and radio in if you need anything. Bud Davis said he'd be glad to help with the stock."

"I can handle it, Dad."

"I know you can, Son."

The trust in her dad's eyes made Kara want to be sick. She knew Greg had been drinking lately. Dad had found beer cans in his truck. How could he trust him alone at the house in Lariat? True, he'd never done anything to harm the stock. But what about himself?

Kara shrugged inwardly. There was nothing she could do about it. There was no way Greg would ever listen to her. *Things were never this mixed up when Mom was alive.* This was not shaping up to be a good day.

Colin pushed back from the table and punched Greg good-naturedly on the arm. "Come on, Ferret Face, we've got a bear to track."

He turned to Dad. "While we're at it we'll check the river trail out past Cedar Ridge. The others are clear. We can even use the one from Pinewood Meadow."

Dad shook his head. "I know you guys got in all right, but we won't need the Pine Creek trail until mid-July. I didn't think we should chance it with clients until then, so I didn't book any ride-ins."

Colin grinned. "You're the boss. Let's go, Greg." He turned and caught Kara's stare.

"You coming, Kara? It might get kinda rough, but from what I hear, Lily can handle it."

It was on the tip of her tongue to tell him just what Lily could handle, when she caught the glint of laughter in his eyes. Her bad mood suddenly lifted. "I can handle any trail you can, Colin Jones. I'll be there in a minute."

She checked to be sure Ryan was helping Anne, then ran to her room and pulled on her boots.

She had Lily almost saddled when Ryan came into the barn. The mare was still fidgety from the night before, and Kara had to stop twice to calm her.

"I'm going too," Ryan demanded. "Saddle Star for me, Colin. Dad said."

Kara could tell Ryan was lying by the way he kept his eyes on the ground. She caught Colin's questioning glance and shook her head. She wanted to swat the little pest but kept her tone casual. "When did Dad tell you that?"

"Just now."

Colin feigned a sudden interest in the cobweb-choked rafters.

Greg wouldn't look at her either. They all knew Dad had gone up to check the water purifier. The tanks were two miles away, and he hadn't been back.

Lily danced sideways and Kara yanked on the lead rope. "HO!" She realized how angry she sounded and lowered her voice.

"Don't lie to me, Ryan Sheridan. You know Dad didn't say you could go. It's too long of a ride and Star wouldn't be able to keep up. Besides, we might run into that bear, and the slowest one would be lunch!"

She knew it was a mean thing to say, but she felt mean. Ryan had deliberately lied to her.

"Lying erodes trust," Mom had often said. "When you lose someone's trust, it's hard to gain it back."

She steeled herself against the tears puddling in her little brother's eyes. "You go back to Anne. Now. We'll talk about this when I get home."

Ryan ran sobbing from the barn.

Colin busied himself with his gelding's saddle, and Kara caught Greg looking at her, a half smile on his face.

"What?" she snapped.

Greg shrugged. "At least you didn't say, 'Just wait until your father gets home.'"

Colin laughed, "Oh, yeah. I used to hate that line."

Kara felt her face turn red. "Well, what was I supposed to do, let him come?"

Greg looked away, but Colin laid a hand on her shoulder. "Hey, lighten up. All kids do that kind of stuff. He'll get over it."

If he meant to cheer her up, it wasn't working. In spite of Lily's energy and the challenging trail, the episode with Ryan left her feeling guilty, like the whole thing was her fault.

# 10

THE TRAIL CROSSED THE WOODEN bridge and wound its way along the far side of the river, dipping into hollows and rising to heights far above the raging water.

They had lost the bear tracks long before they reached the bridge. Kara suspected the ride had just been an excuse for a few hours of freedom before Greg headed back to Lariat and the guests claimed Colin's time for the summer.

She wouldn't have much free time either. Determined to enjoy what was left of the morning, she urged Lily forward, passing Colin in one of the few open spaces and racing up the trail.

She heard Colin yell, and Dakota thundered along behind her. She almost gave Lily another nudge, but they were already going a little too fast for the terrain.

She had just eased the mare into a slow canter, when Dakota moved in alongside and Colin grabbed Lily's right rein. Lily threw her head and sidestepped, nearly unseating her.

Kara pulled the horse to a halt and spun around in the saddle to face Colin. "Don't you ever do that again!" She heard her voice echo across the canyon, but right now she

61

didn't care. "I can control my own horse. You could have gotten me killed!"

Colin backed off, but his face was red with anger. "You nearly killed yourself. There's an S-curve in the trail up ahead. At that speed you'd have galloped right into a tree."

Kara took a deep breath, trying to calm her pounding heart. "Okay. But you could have told me. You never grab another person's reins unless it's an emergency."

"It was an emergency." Colin plucked his hat off his head, wiped his brow with the back of his wrist, and lowered his voice. "I just didn't want you to get hurt, okay? I won't grab Lily again. That's a promise."

He kept his eyes on hers until she turned her head away. He had backed down quickly enough. Why did she feel she was in the wrong?

Greg rode up behind Colin. "Can you two settle this later? I'd like to finish this ride sometime in the next century."

Colin snorted and turned his horse up the trail. Kara followed, and Greg fell in behind. A few yards ahead she saw that Colin was right; there was no way to see the upcoming curves. She shivered. If she had kept up the pace, they'd have run right into a tree, or Lily would have reared and sent them both rolling down into the river.

Once past the curves, Colin put Dakota into a trot. Kara squeezed Lily's sides with her thighs and caught up with him. "Colin. Wait."

He slowed to a walk, and she rode up alongside him. She took a deep breath. "Look, you were right. I'm sorry, okay? I've been in a rotten mood all day."

He tipped his hat. "Apology accepted."

Kara expected him to flash his little-boy grin. When he didn't, she rushed on. "There's something I wanted to ask you. That bumper sticker on your truck. Let go . . ."

"And get a grip on God." He finished it for her.

62

"Yeah. That's it. What does it mean?"

"I heard that at a camp for troubled youths. It's what finally got me going in the right direction and held me together when things got rough."

*Troubled youth? Colin?* "When? Oh, you don't have to talk about it if you don't want to."

He looked over his shoulder where Greg was riding about ten feet behind them. "It's no big deal. Greg's heard it before." He ignored Greg's bored expression and went on. "My folks split when I was fourteen. I couldn't handle it. Dropped out of school, hung around with the wrong crowd. Mom bailed me out three or four times then gave up on me.

"The judge sent me to this camp. The motto was, 'Let go and get a grip on God.' It means let go of whatever's got a grip on you—you know? For me it was anger and grief over my parents' divorce. I learned to let it go and get a grip on God instead."

Kara tried not to show her surprise. She'd never have guessed Colin had been a troublemaker. He didn't go around talking about God all the time, but he didn't go around cussing and fighting like some guys she knew either. She turned back to what he was saying.

"One of the counselors there showed me how God could make a difference in my life."

"What did you do after you got out of . . . uh, youth camp?"

He ducked under a low-hanging tree branch and held it back for Kara to pass. "I went to my uncle in Fairbanks for a couple of years. He ran fishing expeditions in the summer. When I wasn't busy catching up with schoolwork, I went along as guide. Learned a thing or two about the wilderness out there."

"When did you learn to ride?"

"That's how we got around most of the time. Pretty rugged country. The rest I picked up mucking stalls. Until

63

my uncle got sick and decided I'd be better off on the mainland. He e-mailed an old friend, who turned out to be your dad. When your dad offered me this job, I jumped at it."

Kara smiled. *Softhearted Dad.* "What about high school? Did you ever finish?"

"Almost. Only six credits to go. I plan to finish them in the fall. Greg and I will go to the same junior college, only I'll work for your dad during the day and go to school at night."

Colin reached over and tugged at her braid. "Well, Miss Kara, now that you know my life story, are you planning to run me off the ranch?"

Kara laughed. "Maybe." She smacked his hand away and flipped the braid over her shoulder. "The road's pretty straight here. Okay if we canter, Mister Trail Expert?"

He nodded and let her go. By the time he and Greg caught up, she had stopped where the trail ended at an abandoned campsite.

Colin's background surprised her. The part about the youth camp anyway. She needed to think about what he had said. But this wasn't the time or the place.

"Looks like this is the end of the road." She dismounted and led Lily to a patch of knee-high grass. The mare munched contentedly while Kara drank water from her canteen and passed around the oatmeal cookies Anne had handed her just as she was walking out the door.

"This is as far as the horses can go." Colin's mouth was full, and Kara could hardly understand him.

"What do you mean?" She looked around. The campsite was surrounded by thick stands of fir and pine. Berry briers tangled in the underbrush on the other side of the trail, and just below them the swollen river ran twenty yards across.

"I mean," Colin licked his fingers clean of crumbs, "the horses can't go any farther, but once you get past these trees there's a deer trail you can follow on foot."

Kara peered into the brush. "How far does it go?"

Colin shrugged. "Don't know. Greg and I only walked it a couple of miles. Haven't had time to really explore."

She felt a surge of excitement. "Why can't we follow it now? The horses would be okay . . ."

Greg's voice interrupted her. "Hey, it's no skin off my hide, but it's almost one o'clock, and if you guys aren't back to greet the guests, Bossman might get ticked."

Bossman? Kara started to tell Greg off, but settled for a dirty look instead. There had been enough conflict for one day.

"He's right." Colin sounded as disappointed as she was.

She watched him swing into the saddle and turn Dakota's head around in one easy motion. Then he tipped his hat and bowed in her direction. "Next time, ma'am, I'd be happy to escort you down that trail."

Kara fervently hoped there would be a next time. She stowed her canteen and turned Lily's nose toward home.

Back at the lodge, she changed into clean jeans and a colorful V-neck blouse, then headed for the kitchen to find Anne.

The cook was bent over the stove, stirring a pot of fire-starter chili. Kara inhaled the smell of fresh-baked corn bread and remembered she'd had only two oatmeal cookies for lunch.

Anne handed her a stack of bowls. "The boys will be hungry too." She smiled and turned out a whole tin of corn bread into a cloth-lined basket.

Kara felt uneasy as she ladled out the bowls of chili. Anne didn't act any differently after the fuss at the table this morning. *She had to know I was mad.* She wondered if Ryan had said anything about what happened at the barn. She didn't much want to follow through on her talk with him, but she knew she shouldn't let it go.

65

"Is Dad back?"

Anne nodded, then added softly, "Ryan is asleep. Last night was long. For all of us."

Kara felt herself relax. Somehow those few words melted the resentment inside her and made everything seem all right again. She knew she should offer to let Anne ride Lily, but before she could say anything, Colin and Greg stomped through the kitchen door, letting it bang closed behind them.

"Whooee, does that smell good! I'm as hungry as a winter-starved bear." Colin reached for a square of corn bread.

Without thinking, Kara snatched the basket away. "Colin Jones, look at your hands!"

Anne nodded soberly and pointed toward the sink.

Colin grinned and grabbed the bar of Lava soap. "Okay, okay, I guess I know when I'm outnumbered. Boy, you women are bossy!"

Anne laughed, but Kara wanted to crawl under a chair. *There I go again, sounding like my mother!* Colin would never take her seriously.

They had barely finished lunch when the radio crackled to life. Greg hurried into the storeroom and switched on the receiver.

"Eagle Lodge."

Static drowned out the first few words, then the pilot's voice came through. ". . . clouds over here. What's it like on your side? Over."

Greg pushed a button on the mike. "We're clear all the way to the top of the mountain, Mark. Over."

"Okay. Got some company for you. Be there in thirty. Over and out."

**11**

THE REST OF THE DAY went by in a blur of activity. Kara set up the dining room for dinner and gave tours of the property. When one of the guests needed a flashlight and another wanted extra towels, she trooped out to the cabins with the needed supplies.

On Saturday afternoon she started a letter to Tia.

> I almost wish I was back in Lariat cramming for exams. This is hard work. Tonight is the dance. Actually we decided just to play music and let everyone do what they want. I'm going to wear that new outfit Dad bought me. I can't believe I'm so nervous. There's no one to dance with but Colin, and what if he doesn't ask?

At nine o'clock she slipped the silky white blouse over her head and let it settle at her waist. The denim skirt ended just above the knees; short enough to show off the fringed leather boots, but long enough to satisfy Dad.

She leaned backward, shook her head, and combed her fingers through her hair. Anne had fashioned narrow, waist-length braids on each side of her face for her, weaving in thin strands of blue and white leather. She looked more like the first Wakara than ever.

She took a deep breath, opened her bedroom door, and followed the strum of a bass guitar into the main room of the lodge.

A country song echoed through the speakers. Across the room Colin slipped a CD case back into the holder. The guests stood around talking and sipping hot drinks.

Ryan and the Wilson kids were hopping up and down in the middle of the dance floor. "Hey Kara, come and dance. Jenny really knows how." Ryan's voice carried over the music, and she wanted to clamp her hand over his mouth.

Everyone stopped talking, and one of the men gave a low whistle. They were all looking at her. The overhead lights were bright. Her face was on fire, and she felt suddenly light-headed. *Oh, God, please don't let me faint.* She couldn't run back to her room. That would look so . . .

Dad's arm circled her shoulders. "You look wonderful, Sugar Bear. Anne saved you a diet Coke. It's in the fridge."

*Mom would be proud of you.* He didn't say it, but she could hear it in his voice. Instead of making her sad, she felt happier than she had in months.

The music changed to a slower song. She looked up and saw Colin walking toward her. He had changed into a colorful, long-sleeved shirt, black Wranglers, and freshly polished boots. When he got closer she could smell his aftershave.

"Want to show these city folk how to dance?"

She nodded and took his outstretched hand.

Colin's two-step was smooth. "You look nice, Wakara." He reached up and drew one thin braid over her shoulder. "Like a real Indian princess."

She looked for the teasing laughter in his eyes. It wasn't there. *He's serious.* For some reason that made her nervous.

She decided to lighten the moment. "I am an Indian princess, Colin Jones. And don't you forget it."

He smiled then, and the rest of the evening was fun. She danced with Dad and Ryan, then three more times with Colin. By midnight she was exhausted but too excited to sleep.

Dad had hustled Ryan off to bed hours ago. When the guests had all gone back to their cabins, Colin yawned and stretched. "Guess I'd better turn in too. Got some folks who want to ride early tomorrow, and your dad's going to have a church service at seven o'clock."

Kara groaned. "Sunday's supposed to be my day off. You'd think I'd be able to sleep in."

"You can." Colin's grin was back. "You can sleep 'til six o'clock instead of five." He leaned down and kissed her on the forehead. "You're a great dancer, Wakara. Thanks."

She caught her breath. By the time she thought to say, "Good night, Colin, I had fun too," he was already out the door.

Back in her room, she picked up her letter to Tia.

> What a night. Colin is an awesome dancer. Sometimes I think he really likes me. I wish I could figure out how I feel about him.

All night long, in her dreams, the music played while she and Colin danced. When the alarm went off at six, she wondered if anything about last night had been real.

At breakfast Colin gobbled his food, then grabbed his jacket and headed out the door. "Gotta get the horses saddled. A few of the men are going fishing upriver, but the rest of the group want to ride." He was gone before Kara could say good morning.

Greg tossed his napkin on the table. "I'm outta here. Mark, you ready?"

The pilot nodded. "Sure, but why the hurry? The ranch isn't going anywhere."

Greg just glared at him and stalked off. He came back with his bulging sports bag and dropped it with a thud at the front door.

Mark shrugged and downed the last of his coffee. "Great meal, Ms. Lightfoot. You're the best cook in the state." He kissed her cheek, and her face darkened in a blush.

Dad laughed. "Watch out, Mark, she'll have you fat as a summer hog in no time."

"What's a summer hog? Hey, save some bacon for me!" Ryan scrambled into his chair and snatched the last two pieces off the plate.

"You're the summer hog, Ryan Sheridan. Use some manners."

Dad interrupted. "It's all right, Wakara. Everyone else is done." He watched her with a puzzled look on his face.

Ryan ignored her as Anne spooned eggs and fried potatoes onto his plate.

Kara fumed silently. *He doesn't say a word when Greg's acting like a jerk, but I say one little thing and it's lecture time.*

After the guests had finished eating, Kara helped with the dishes. She felt uncomfortable. Dad hadn't really lectured her. *Get over it, Wako. It's no big deal.*

"I will go to Otter Lake this morning." Anne handed her another plate.

*Uh-oh. Now she'll ask to borrow Lily.* Kara cringed. She had wanted to ride Lily herself this morning.

But the cook went on, "Do you like to fish?"

"What? Oh, sure. There's some pretty nice trout up there."

"I would like company."

Kara didn't know what to say. Was Anne inviting her along? If so, who would ride Lily?

70

It was almost like the woman could read her thoughts. "Colin will leave the buckskin for me."

"The buckskin? You mean Dakota? What's Colin riding?"

Anne grinned. "The Appaloosa. She will learn some manners today, I think."

"But Dakota's huge. And spirited. No one but Colin ever rides him."

"He has a kind eye."

Kara blinked. Anne was teasing her. Suddenly they both laughed, and the older woman tugged on one of Kara's slender braids.

"You are pretty when you smile, Little Moon. Last night you looked beautiful. Many people noticed."

Kara shrugged. A lot of good it did. Colin hadn't even looked at her this morning.

By ten o'clock the chores were done. The men staying in cabin four had shouldered their fishing poles and headed upriver right after breakfast. The others, including Ryan, had all gone on a trail ride.

The Wilson boy had been taking lessons and could ride better than they had thought. Colin had put him on one of the older horses and let Ryan tag along on Star.

Kara hummed some of last night's music as she saddled Lily for the ride to Otter Lake. With Ryan out of her hair and Anne busy fishing, she'd finally have some time to herself.

Anne handed her a long, tubelike cardboard case. "Fishing rods," she explained.

There were no reels, only a net on a long pole. Kara tied the gear onto Lily's saddle, then watched as Anne slipped a bridle over Dakota's ears, grabbed a handful of mane, and leapt onto the horse's back.

Kara realized her mouth was hanging open and snapped it shut. "You're riding bareback?"

71

"My father never allowed us to burden a horse with a saddle. Without it, horse and rider work together, become as one." She clucked lightly with her tongue, and the big horse moved calmly toward the trail.

Kara felt a flash of irritation. *Is there anything that woman can't do?* Anne was right. Bareback was easier on the horse. And the rider. Kara had ridden that way often, but only from the pasture to the barn. Anyway, stirrups and a saddle were safer for a trail.

She followed slowly, enjoying the feel of the sun on her back as they followed the river east, crossed the meadow, and headed into the trees. Thunderheads were already building up over the mountains in the north.

The storms came almost every day this time of year, but they seldom hit until late afternoon. Luckily, they were always accompanied by rain. Kara still felt skittish when the lightning flashed. She had seen what dry lightning could do. It was that kind of storm that had killed her mother.

# 12

THEY MADE THE HALF-HOUR ride to the lake in silence. Kara tied the horses in a stand of fir trees, then helped Anne carry the gear down the steep, fern-covered slope. The lake was fed by two creeks and an underground spring. It was small, but deep enough to shelter schools of rainbow trout and smallmouth bass.

They turned over stones at the water's edge, uncovering hellgrammites—Ryan called them skitter bugs—to use as bait. Then they rigged and set the lines.

"Now, we wait." Anne settled cross-legged on a large, flat rock and began digging through her backpack. She pulled out two books and handed one to Kara.

"Here is my father's book about the Yana people. It is yours."

"Mine? But why would your father want to give his book away?"

"My father left it to me, so it is mine to give."

Kara studied the cover. It would be great to learn more about the people Anne thought were her ancestors, but could she really accept part of someone else's inheritance?

"A gift freely given should at least be considered."

Kara blushed and took the book. "Thanks, I'd love to read it."

Anne nodded and picked up the book she'd brought for herself. Kara recognized it right away. "Mom had a Bible just like that."

Anne rubbed her fingers across the frayed edges of the soft, red leather. "It is my favorite. Small enough to carry anywhere." She grinned. "Worship and fishing keep good company."

Kara couldn't help but grin back. "Riding too. Sometimes I pray while I'm riding Lily. When I'm alone, in the woods or by the river, God always seems so close."

"Do you know Jesus, Wakara?"

The question felt like a slap. "Of course I do! I accepted Him when I was Ryan's age." She realized she was shouting, but the older woman ignored her tone of voice.

"And He is close only in the woods?"

She shrugged. "Well, yeah. I guess lately, not even then."

Anne just looked at her, waiting, and she stumbled on. "Actually, He hasn't been around much at all since He let my mother die. And you know what? I really don't care!" She swiped at the tears flooding her eyes, then spun around and walked quickly up the footpath that led around the lake.

The path twisted and climbed. She stumbled over a tree root, caught herself, then stopped to catch her breath. *Yes, you do care, and you know it.* Her conscience nagged. *And anyway, it's not Anne's fault. She asks you one simple question and you explode.*

"What's wrong with me?" she whispered. "I've been acting like a total jerk. And I don't even know why."

The wind picked up, raining pine needles over her shoulders and hair. Thunder boomed in the distance. She broke into a jog just as lightning flashed across the darkening sky.

74

When she reached the spot where she'd left Anne, the woman wasn't there.

For a moment Kara panicked. Would Anne go off and leave her?

Lily whinnied. Kara climbed the steep bank and found Anne waiting. She had stored the gear and was already on Dakota's back, holding Lily's reins.

Rain dripped in big, fat drops down the back of her shirt. Once again she let Dakota take the lead. He set a fast pace, but by the time they got home she was soaked to the skin.

For the rest of the day, she felt as snarly as a bear in a bees' nest. She helped clean a dozen plump rainbow trout, brushed and fed Lily, then dragged herself up the hill to the lodge. She was supposed to change and set the tables for dinner, but by the time she got to the kitchen her stomach was doing flips.

It didn't help when she caught Ryan sneaking out of the storage room. "Hold it, Kiddo." He tried to make a run for it, but she stepped in front of him. "What were you doing in there? If you were messing with that radio again, Dad's going to have your hide."

He glared at her. "Dad showed me how. I was just practicing."

"Who did you call?" she demanded.

"Nobody." His eyes watered. "Let me go, or I'll tell Dad you're being mean."

He pushed past her, head high, fists clenched at his sides. Kara watched him march out of the room and felt like crying herself.

*What's going on around here? Everything's falling apart.* Ryan had been more than a pest lately. He'd been a total pain, and she didn't know what to do about it. Dad had enough problems without having to deal with a bratty six-year-old.

That was supposed to be her responsibility, but lately it was like nothing she did was right.

Anne came in with a dishpan full of fish from the freezer. "We will grill trout tonight. With what we caught today, there is enough."

Just the thought of fish made Kara's stomach churn. She dashed through the kitchen door and into the bath shed. When she returned, she was shaking all over.

Anne felt her forehead. "Ouch! You are hotter than my oven. Can you walk to your room?"

Kara nodded, but she wasn't at all sure she could make it without being sick again.

When she finally lay down, the room began to spin. Someone laid a cool cloth across her head. She opened her eyes. Anne was there with an empty pail and a pan of water. The woman lifted her head gently and slid another damp cloth behind her neck.

"Sleep now. I will be back."

This time the dream was more frightening than ever.

*Mom was running through the smoke, heading back into the fire, but this time Kara followed. She ran and ran, calling out until she thought her lungs would burst from the heat and smoke. Mom had disappeared. Kara dropped to her knees. The ground beneath her turned to soggy ashes. From a distance she could hear Mom calling her, but when she tried to move she just sank deeper into the mire.*

"Wakara." Not Mom's voice. "Wakara, wake up now."

Anne. Kara opened her eyes. And Dad. To her relief, the room stayed still.

"Sit up a little." Dad's hand on her back eased her forward as he slid another pillow behind her head. "There, do you feel any better?"

Kara nodded and realized it was true. Her stomach wasn't churning, and she didn't feel as hot. But when she tried to talk she sounded like a cross between a bullfrog and a mouse.

"My throat," she managed to croak.

Anne moved to her side. "Drink this. It will give you strength."

Kara took the mug Anne offered her and sniffed the steaming liquid. Peppermint. And chamomile. She couldn't tell what else. Anne waited patiently while she blew on the tea to cool it, then sipped. The warm brew eased the tightness in her throat, and the sweetness soothed her stomach. "Good," she managed.

The cook nodded. "The herbs will help you heal." She tucked the covers around Kara's waist. "Rest now."

Her father felt her forehead for the tenth time and peered into her eyes. "You've been out of it for sixteen hours. Anne hasn't slept. We've been taking turns watching you and calling in your symptoms on the radio. Doctor Glenn is convinced you have the flu, but if we hadn't been able to rouse you this morning, Mark was going to fly him in."

Kara groaned. All this trouble because of her. She felt sleepy and disoriented. Sixteen hours. It must be Monday morning. More guests would check in this afternoon. She had to get up. There were cabins to be cleaned, and Anne needed her help in the dining room. But she felt so weak. She gave in and closed her eyes.

When she opened them again, Ryan was sitting on the foot of her bed, his baseball cards spread out all over the covers.

"Ry?"

He jumped, then grinned. "Hi, Kara. It's my turn to sit with you." His teeth crunched something, and she detected the faint smell of butterscotch. "Dad said not to get too close. You might be catchy."

She tried to laugh but had to settle for a smile.

"It's okay. Dad said not to make you talk. I'm supposed to go get him if you wake up." He pushed up on his knees and peered into her eyes. "Are you really awake, Kara? Dad said you might hall-ucin-gate—then I'm supposed to run."

Kara did laugh then, but even to her own ears she sounded like a tortured mule. Ryan jumped off the bed and fled, leaving behind a trail of candy wrappers and baseball cards.

It was Wednesday before she could stand up long enough to take a shower. By the time she dressed and dried her hair, her intentions to get back to work faded. The best she could do was sit at the counter in the kitchen and watch Anne prepare lunch.

"Your strength will return," the cook assured her. "Then I will sleep for a week." She flashed Kara a teasing smile.

"Thanks for taking care of me," Kara voiced her thoughts. "And for doing all the chores. You must be tired."

Anne nodded. "A little." She pushed a pan of biscuits into the oven, then lifted the lid on a pot of vegetable beef stew.

Kara's mouth watered, and she realized she was actually hungry again.

Without asking, the cook poured a ladle full of stew into a bowl and set it in front of Kara. "Ryan dries dishes and can lay a fire."

For some reason the words stung, but Kara could see no hint of scolding on Anne's face.

She had been pretty tough on Ry lately. Her conscience had been prodding her for weeks. *But,* she reminded herself, *most of the time he asks for it. Lying. Fooling with the radio. Refusing to listen when I tell him to do something.*

She frowned. "How do you get him to help? I never can."

Anne handed her a napkin. "I raised five brothers."

Kara almost dropped her spoon. "Five!"

The woman shrugged. "Our father worked hard."

Kara was curious. Anne talked a lot about her father. She had mentioned a brother back at Thurston Springs. He was the one who'd found the book on the Yana tribe at Anne's house and sent it to her on one of Mark's charter flights. But she hadn't ever said a word about her mother. Kara was about to ask when Anne spoke.

"Our mother died when I was ten."

"Oh." Kara wasn't sure what to say. "I'm sorry."

She wanted to continue the conversation, but just then the screen door slammed twice and the babble of voices coming from the dining room sent Anne into a flurry of activity.

# 13

DURING THE NEXT FEW WEEKS, the summer weather ignited an explosion of guests. The cabins were booked solid, and there was always something to be done. Twice Kara started to read the book Anne's father had written, but she had to put it down after only a few paragraphs.

One afternoon in late July, she actually found time to write Tia.

> Be glad you're not here. It's so hot even the lizards are looking for shade! It hasn't rained in weeks, and everything's turning a yucky brown. But none of the guests seem to mind. They all lay around the deck getting fried. Pretty dumb, huh?
>
> Colin had to stop the afternoon trail rides. He does mornings and that's it. I haven't seen much of him lately, but he asked if I'd ride with him tomorrow. There's a couple of really novice riders, and he could use some backup. I can't believe how psyched I am. I'd really like to go out with him. For real, you know?

Kara put down her pen. There wasn't much chance of that. They were way too busy, and there was always a mob of people around. Besides, she knew Dad wouldn't let her go on a real date. Not until she turned sixteen.

She addressed the envelope, then slipped into her sandals. If Mark was still at the lodge he could take the letter to Tia now.

She crossed the empty rec room and opened the front door. One look told her Mark's plane had gone. She heard the rumble of thunder in the distance, then a flash lit up the eastern sky.

"Dry lightning."

Anne was standing at the wall of windows in the dining room and staring off across the mountains. She nodded and handed Kara the newspaper Mark had brought in that morning from Lariat. "The devil's matches."

Kara read the headline out loud: "Fire Destroys Wildlife Refuge."

Below the caption was a picture of several volunteers herding small animals into cages. A firefighter, his face black with soot, held an injured raccoon.

Dad walked up behind them. "It'll get worse unless we get some rain." He looked at Anne. "I don't want to frighten either of you, but we need to be careful, even with the barbecue. And we should practice an evacuation plan."

For the rest of the week they monitored the radio. So far fires burned in Idaho, California, and southern Oregon, nothing close enough to worry about, but Dad cautioned the guests not to roam too far and told Colin to cancel the trail rides. "It's too hot for the horses anyway."

Kara tried to hide her disappointment, but Anne picked up on it right away. "There will be other rides. This will not last."

By the second week in August, the afternoon thunderstorms had stopped, and they had two days of steady rain. Dad turned off the radio. "Fires are under control."

"We will have barbecue tonight," Anne announced as she dug packages of steak out of the freezer.

"All right!" Ryan raced for the door. "I get to dump the charcoal in the pit."

Kara laughed. "Slow down, Ry. We have to dig out the old ashes first."

Colin was reaching for his hat. "Can you do that later? The horses need exercise, and I could use some help checking out the trail to Otter Lake."

Ryan spun around and planted himself in front of Colin. "I can come."

Kara bit her lip and launched a pleading look at Dad.

To her relief he actually got the message. "Uh, hold on, Tiger, I think Colin and Kara can handle it. Come on, I'll help you dig out the barbecue pit."

She didn't have any trouble reading the look Dad flashed her as he led Ryan out the door. It said "Behave yourself," loud and clear. Any other time she might have been insulted. Right now she was too excited to care.

She wasn't the only one excited. Lily pranced and jigged the whole time Kara was trying to saddle her. She finally had to resort to crossties to get the job done.

Colin laughed. "Dakota's not much better. They've been cooped up too long, and they're telling us about it. I think we'd better give them a workout in the meadow before we try the trail."

She kept a tight rein until they reached the meadow. The ground had absorbed most of the rain, leaving only a few muddy spots. "If we avoid these holes, we'll be fine," she called to Colin. "Let's jog them in a circle."

He nodded, and Kara took the lead, putting Lily into a slow jog, then a canter. They went around twice in each direction, then she gave Lily her head. The mare needed little encouragement to run, and Dakota was all too happy to follow her.

Colin moved alongside her, and they rode together. The wind on her face, the rhythm of hooves like drumbeats on the hard-packed ground, Lily's muscles bunching and unfolding beneath her—for one wild moment Kara wished they could go on like this forever.

Too soon, Colin slowed Dakota to a canter, then a trot. Kara took the cue and followed. When they finally brought the horses to a walk, she sighed and gave the command to stop.

"Whooee," Colin shouted, "that was some ride!" Sweat made muddy rivulets down his face, and his hat had fallen over one ear. He looked like he'd just wrestled a bull.

Kara grinned. "It sure was, but you almost lost your hat."

"At least I didn't lose my hair."

"What?" Kara felt herself redden at his teasing laughter, then realized the hair she had braided and coiled on top of her head had slipped to one side. She tried to straighten it but couldn't find the plastic clip she'd used to fasten it that morning.

Colin leaned over and brushed a speck of dirt from her face, then reached up and pulled out the final pin. The braid tumbled down her back, coming half undone. "Let it fall, Indian Princess. Your hair's too beautiful to hide."

He smiled, then turned Dakota's head toward the trail.

For a few seconds, Kara couldn't move. Did he think she was beautiful, or just her hair? She shook her head and loosened the rest of the braid. *Cut it out, Wako, he didn't mean anything by it.*

She clicked to Lily and followed Colin up the trail. Except for one steep, muddy slope, the path was clear all the way to the Pine Creek trail junction.

Back at the barn, they brushed the horses down. Kara gave them each a flake of hay, while Colin filled the five-gallon buckets with fresh water. As they were leaving he asked, "See you tonight?"

She fumbled with the latch on Lily's stall. "What's tonight?"

"Square dance. A last minute thing. Laura Anderson's father is a caller." He swept his hat across his chest and gave a mock bow. "I'd be mighty pleased, Miz Sheridan, if you'd save a round for me."

"Maybe."

"Keep 'em guessing," Tia had said. "It's the only way to survive the boyfriend zone."

Kara steeled herself against the confusion on Colin's face. "Thanks for the ride." She turned away and forced herself to walk casually toward the lodge.

Had she hurt his feelings? Of course she had hurt his feelings. He'd probably never ask her to do anything with him again. So what? *So, I like him.* At least, she liked him when he wasn't acting like a clown.

She had always thought having a boyfriend would be fun. Well, she was sure making a mess of it. *Oh, Mom, I wish you were here. I need to talk to you, bad.*

*Just relax, Wakara, be yourself.* Kara swiped her wrist across her burning eyes. How many times had she heard that one? Maybe she should listen this time. It just might be good advice.

# 14

KARA PLACED THE LAST of the steak knives on table five, then scanned the area to be sure the floor was clean. There was space for twenty people in the dining room. The cabins only held sixteen, but they often had extras like Mark, or friends from Lariat who dropped in for the day.

She straightened the chairs, then headed for her room to change. That red cotton top, she decided, and her wrap-around skirt. Would she get to dance with Colin? He probably wasn't even speaking to her, and she couldn't blame him.

As she passed the kitchen doorway, she heard the crackle, buzz of the radio signaling a call. She shrugged. Anne would get it. The crackling stopped, but it was Ryan's voice she heard.

"Eagle Lodge. Who's this?"

Kara sighed and hurried to the radio room. "Ryan Sheridan, you know you're not supposed to play in here. Give me that mike."

He scrambled away from her. "Here she is." He tossed the microphone in her direction. "It's Tia-wee-a the big fat heehaw."

Kara caught the mike and glowered at him. "You're in trouble, Bud. And quit acting like a baby."

"Ryan? Kara? All right you guys, who's there?"

"I'm here, Tia."

"Good, it's you. Pops gave me three minutes to talk to you, and I wasted two of them getting past that goofball brother of yours."

"Sorry."

"Whoot whoot whoot." Ryan crouched in the doorway, curling his upper lip, scratching his armpits, and making noise like an orangutan.

"Don't worry. When I get off the radio, he's bear meat." She glared at him again, then turned her back. "So what's up? Over."

"My History grade, that's what's up. To a B! Aren't you proud of me? Over."

"Proud? Tia, that's awesome. When did you find out? Over."

"Just this morning. Pops almost expired. For a reward I get to take the rest of the summer off. Cool, huh?"

There was a pause and some static, but before Kara could say anything else, Tia was back. "Uh, Kara? Is your dad coming out anytime soon? Over."

"I don't know. Why? Over."

"Oh, I just wondered."

"Come on, Tia. What's going on? Is something wrong?"

"No. Yes. I mean, I really want to see you and I thought maybe if your dad was coming . . ."

Kara felt a chill run through her. "Is it Greg?"

The line crackled, and she thought for a minute Tia had cut out. Then she heard her friend's whisper over the static. "Yeah. He's really weirding out, Kara. I'm totally freaked for him. He's been running with T. J. Magic's friends. Everyone knows those guys are, like, strung out all the time.

"Uh-oh. I gotta go. Pops is gonna go ballistic if I don't get off. Look, just get your dad to come home soon, okay? Bye."

The line popped, then hummed. Tia had cut out.

Kara felt cold all over. Empty and sad and angry all at the same time. She walked to the window and leaned on the sill. Now what? Tell Dad and ruin his week, or keep quiet and let Greg ruin his life? There really wasn't a choice.

She'd tell Dad tonight, when the guests had gone back to their cabins and Ryan was in bed. Ryan. She'd get on him about the radio later. This was no time to cause more of a fuss.

In spite of her mood, the steak, baked potato, and green salad tasted good. Everyone else must have thought so too, because there wasn't a scrap left on anyone's plate.

Dad wiped his mouth with a napkin and pushed away from the table. "Fantastic meal, Anne."

He turned to Colin. "We'll wait until later to start the entertainment. Why don't you turn the horses out, then take a breather? I promised Ryan I'd help him polish his boots."

When the men left, Anne started rinsing dishes. Kara followed her to the sink with an armload of plates, still wondering how to tell Dad about Greg.

"You are troubled."

The cook's voice startled her, and she quickly set the dishes on the counter. "Is it that obvious?"

"Maybe not to all. I see the wookawkaw sitting on your shoulder."

"The what?"

"The woodpecker picks and picks at the wounded tree. If someone does not chase it away, eventually the tree will die."

Kara shook her head. "You can't chase this one away. Greg's headed for real trouble, and I don't know what to do."

87

Anne nodded. "Greg is wounded. Like you, he bleeds, but in a different way."

Kara leaned against the sink. "You mean over Mom?"

Instead of answering, Anne dried her hands and moved back toward the table. She pulled out two chairs and sat in one. Kara hesitated, then took the other. Anne didn't talk much, but what she did have to say was usually important. It wouldn't hurt to listen.

But the cook was silent. It looked like she was praying. When she finally spoke, Kara had to strain to hear.

"When wetyetmas, the goose, loses her mate, she calls and calls. She does not believe he is gone. She waits and waits for his return. When he does not come, she paces and cries. She pecks at other geese that dare to venture near. Finally, she accepts that she is alone and flies away to join the others on the pond."

Kara had to bite her lip to keep from crying. "You mean like grief. My counselor talked about the stages. Disbelief, denial, anger, and acceptance. She said we have to go through it all before the pain gets better."

Anne nodded. "You have listened well. But not everyone moves from one to the other at the same time. And sometimes people get stuck. If wetyetmas does not move on, if she ruffles her feathers and refuses to let the others near, she will soon starve and grow too weak to fly."

Kara's eyes stung. After Mom died, Greg had helped Dad with the arrangements. He had gone to the celebration service and the cemetery, but she hadn't once seen him cry. Afterward he went away by himself for a week. He'd been sullen and angry ever since.

It was easy to see how Greg could be stuck. Dad still cried, but he was trying to move on. When she thought about it, so was Ryan. He hadn't said a word about Mom since Anne arrived.

Where did that put her?

Kara started to speak, then changed her mind. She didn't want to even think about that question, let alone ask Anne. Something told her she wouldn't like the answer.

Anne laid a gentle hand on her head, then moved back to the sink. "It will be dark soon. You will want to wash and change. I will finish in here."

"Thanks, Anne." She hesitated, then walked over and gave her a hug. "For everything."

## 15

THE THERMOMETER IN THE rec room read 90 degrees, and the square dance petered out after two rounds. The only ones who seemed to be having a good time were Colin and Laura.

Laura Anderson. Tall and perky, with cropped blond hair and a peaches-and-cream complexion that had probably never seen the sun. She had latched onto Colin like a lasso on a bull, and Colin had a ring in his nose before he knew it.

Dad walked by with a stack of almost empty popcorn bowls and interrupted Kara's thoughts. "What would you say to a couple of days in Lariat?"

She nearly dropped the bag of empty pop cans she was carrying to the kitchen. "What? You mean that?"

Dad laughed. "If I had known you'd be that eager, I'd have tried to arrange it sooner." His smile faded. "Are you doing okay, Wakara? You've been working pretty hard. I know it's been a while since you've had a break."

His voice sounded raspy, and he cleared his throat. "Uh, I've been wanting to tell you how much I appreciate all you do for us. With your mother gone, I couldn't . . . Well, I just couldn't get along without you, Sweetheart. You know that, don't you?"

Kara felt the tears sting her eyes. She wrapped her arms around his waist and buried her face against his damp cotton shirt. His hug was strong and comforting. When his breath caught on a sob, she couldn't hold back.

Dad held her for a few minutes while they both cried, then he dropped a kiss on her hair and pushed her gently away. "Well, as your mom would say, I guess we needed that."

She nodded, not trusting herself to speak, and grabbed a napkin from the box on the serving counter to blow her nose. Dad pulled a clean kerchief from his back pocket and did the same. They looked at each other and laughed.

"It's going to be a slow week. The guests will all be gone by noon tomorrow, and there are no more scheduled until Saturday morning. Colin and Anne can hold down the fort for awhile."

He patted her cheek. "Get some sleep, Sugar Bear. We'll tell Ryan in the morning."

Her first thought after he had gone was, *Thank you, God.* They were going home, and she hadn't even had to mention Greg. Now maybe Dad could find out for himself, and she wouldn't have to be involved.

*Coward.* Dad was hurting enough already. Now he had to find out his oldest son was in trouble. She thought about Greg's sullen attitude. He was barely civil to anyone, and more than once she'd smelled beer on his breath, but he'd never done anything really horrible. Maybe it wasn't as bad as Tia said.

Between Colin and Greg, her mind was spinning. But the crying must have done her some good, because her head had barely hit the pillow before she was out.

The next morning they took off right after breakfast and landed in Lariat before the sun was high.

Kara had just unpacked her overnight bag when her bedroom door flew open, and Tia launched herself into the room. "All right! You brought your new outfit. The youth group at church rented Rodeo City for Wednesday night. Free pop, and hamburgers or chicken sandwiches for a buck."

Kara groaned. "Tia Sanchez, I love you to pieces, but I came home for a rest. Do you have the days planned too?"

"Of course. I knew you wouldn't have Lily, so I asked Mom and she said you could ride her mare." Tia flopped down on the bed beside her. "Tomorrow we go shopping. Then I have a big surprise!"

Tia's enthusiasm was contagious. Kara felt relaxed and happy. "What's the big surprise?"

Tia sat up. "You know that B in History? Well, Mom said I could go to the Beauty Palace. Haircut, nails, the works. And when I heard you were coming I told her, 'Only if Kara comes too,' and would you believe it? She said yes. No argument. Isn't that cool?"

"Uh, yeah, that's cool, but I don't know."

"Don't know what? Come on, Kara, it's the ultimate deal. We get complete makeovers and Mom pays for the whole thing."

Kara looked at her short, clean fingernails. "It does sound like fun, but isn't it kind of a waste? The nails won't last long with my job."

"So what? At least you'll have them for Wednesday night." Tia studied her own ragged cuticles. "Trevor Sanders was asking if you'd be there."

"Trevor Sanders? Isn't he the guy who won the regional High School Rodeo finals?"

"Up close and personal. That is, unless you and Colin…?"

Kara didn't like the gleam in Tia's eyes. She shook her head. "There is no me and Colin. We're just friends." Well, they were if he hadn't crossed her off his list completely after last night.

"So how are you gonna get your hair cut?"

"Whoa! Who said anything about cutting my hair?"

"Oh, I don't know. I just thought you might want a change. Like a new look, you know? I'm going to get mine cropped. Jennifer Hall had hers done two weeks ago. It's awesome."

"No way is anybody going to cut my hair!" Kara glanced into the mirror on her dresser, but instead of her own image, Laura Anderson's blond bob flashed into her mind.

Kara shivered. Did she dare cut off her hair? What would Dad say? Hadn't he always told her she could wear her hair and clothes any way she wanted? Within limits, sure. But getting a haircut was no big deal. Once again her mind flashed a picture of Laura. And Jennifer Hall had been prom queen two years in a row.

She took a deep breath. "Okay, you're on!"

Tia looked at her like she was on fire. "You mean, you'll do it?"

Kara nodded and held out her hand. "Lead me to the slaughter."

Tia giggled. "Tomorrow morning. Nine o'clock. Be there."

Tia's mom honked the horn at eight-thirty the next morning. Kara swallowed the last bite of toast, grabbed her backpack, and sprinted out the door.

A few minutes later she watched as Tia's dark brown hair fell around her, landing in heaps on the floor. When the stylist brought out the clippers, Kara cringed, but Tia just giggled, then grinned into the mirror. Her hair was shaped shorter in back, long enough on the sides to swish when she bent her head forward or moved it side to side.

"Wow. I'm gonna like this. I feel ten pounds lighter." She hopped out of the chair. "Your turn. Come on, Kara, you're gonna love it."

Kara suddenly felt dizzy. It wasn't too late; she could still back out. Her knees felt about as strong as Play-Doh, so she sat while the stylist undid her braid and brushed out her long, black hair. It fell to her waist even when she pulled it over her shoulder.

A whole new image. She took a deep breath and closed her eyes. She could picture the look on Colin's face when he smoothed the long, slender braid at the dance. "You look like an Indian princess," he had said. She opened her eyes and saw the stylist frowning at her in the mirror.

"Are you sure you want to do this?"

Kara shook her head. The woman smiled. "Tell you what. We'll just put it up like this." She twisted the hair into a swirling mass on top of Kara's head. She pinned it into place and pulled several long strands free, curling them into spirals against Kara's neck and cheeks.

Half a can of hair spray later, Kara took the hand mirror and studied the results. The mirror reflected a young woman—suave, sophisticated, and looking several years older than fifteen. She smiled. "Rodeo City, here I come."

"It's awesome, Kara." Tia flashed her bright red nails in the direction of the sidewalk. "Let's go to Henry's for lunch. My treat."

"No way. I can pay for my own. Dad gave me a check for the work I've done this summer." She suddenly felt adventuresome, free. And she was beginning to like the tendrils of hair brushing against her cheeks.

"Why don't we go to The Hut instead? Maybe we'll see some of the gang from school," Kara said.

"All right. Maybe Trevor will be there." Tia flashed her a sneaky grin.

Kara laughed. "Yeah, maybe he will. And maybe he'll go with the youth group to Rodeo City. And maybe Devon Andrews will tag along with you."

Tia's mom picked them up in front of the beauty shop at three o'clock. They drove slowly past the fields and farms on the outskirts of Lariat. The road curved uphill into patches of evergreen trees, many of them blackened and bare from last year's fire.

When they came to the curve where her mother's car had gone off the road, Kara forced herself to look away. She didn't need to spoil her good mood. Anyway, Mom wasn't down there in those woods. She was safe in heaven.

Mom had told her about that from the time she was old enough to listen. "If you believe that Jesus is God, that He died for your sins and rose again, then you don't have to be afraid to die." And she did believe. She had accepted that gift a long time ago.

At the funeral Pastor Taylor had told them, "The Bible says we will grieve, but not like those who have no hope." She could almost feel the pressure of his hand on her shoulder. "You have hope, Wakara, because your mom belonged to God. And when she died, she went instantly into His presence."

*But what about us? We're the ones who suffer because she's not here.*

They turned down the gravel drive and pulled up in front of the house. Kara waved a final thank you to Mrs. Sanchez and Tia, then went through the side door into the family room. Ryan had his face just inches away from the TV, watching John Wayne swagger down the main street of some dusty western town.

"Back up, Ry. You're sitting way too close."

He scooted back an inch, then turned to look at her. "Kara?"

He scrambled to his feet. "Whooee! Dad! Come quick." She could still hear him hollering as he ran out of the room. "Dad! You gotta see this. Kara got beautified!"

# 16

RODEO CITY WAS SO CROWDED, the girls almost missed Trevor and Devon, who stood waiting for them just inside the door. It took an hour to get their sandwiches.

The youth leader, Mr. Andrews, warned them that only line dancing was allowed, but they could also use the pool tables and the mechanical bull.

After showing off by riding the bull a full eight seconds, Trevor threw an arm over Kara's shoulders. "Whew, this place is jammed. What you say we vacate to somewhere a little more private?"

He winked at her, and Kara winced. He'd been coming on like that all evening, grabbing her hand and trying to kiss her. She was getting really tired of fighting him off. To make matters worse, Mr. Andrews was watching them like a hawk.

"I don't think so." She shrugged his arm away. "My dad's picking us up at eleven."

Usually she hated having Dad pick her up from parties, but tonight she was actually glad she couldn't drive.

At five to eleven, the guys walked them outside. Kara took a deep breath. "Boy, it feels good to breathe fresh air."

"Aren't you cold?" Trevor slipped his arm around her shoulders again.

"Not a bit." Kara pulled away just as her father's dark blue Trooper turned the corner. "Look, Tia, there's Dad. Let's meet him on the corner so he doesn't have to park."

"Got ya." Tia took Kara's arm. "Bye, guys. Thanks for dinner. I'll talk to you later, Dev, okay?"

Kara caught the glare in Trevor's eyes and decided not to say anything more. Instead, she flagged down Dad, and she and Tia piled into the backseat.

"Whoa! Intense," they said at the same time. Kara caught Dad's frown in the rearview mirror.

He looked back at the guys standing on the sidewalk. "Everything okay, girls?"

She didn't turn around. "Sure, Dad, we're fine."

She was glad when he dropped his gaze and pulled out onto the boulevard. "I saw your dad at the grange tonight, Tia. He said you could come back to Eagle Lodge with us for the last week of the season," he said, grinning back at them. "That is, if you want to."

Tia grabbed Kara's arm. "Awesome! I mean, sure, Mr. Sheridan, I'd love to come—if it's all right with Kara and everything."

Kara rolled her eyes. "Tia, you're a nut case. Of course I want you to come. Besides, I could use some help cleaning cabins. You can do the bathrooms."

Kara felt happier than she had in weeks. It would be great to have Tia at the lodge. She went to bed thinking about the trails they could explore. Tia couldn't bring Patches, of course, but Colin would find her a good horse out of the string.

*Colin.* Laura Anderson was gone by now. Would Colin be moping around like a love-starved calf?

*Don't be too hard on him, Wako. At least he's not an octopus like Trevor Sanders.* She shivered. If she never saw him again, it would be too soon.

97

She turned on her side, cuddled her pillow, and drifted into a pleasant dream.

*She and Lily were cantering across an open meadow. The wind kicked up warm, earthy smells, ruffling Lily's mane and making her own long hair fly. Running free.*

*A huge, black cloud hovered over the tops of the mountains.*

*Great-grandmother rode beside her. She was shouting something, trying to be heard over the thunder of hooves and the roaring wind. "You are not Nez Perce."*

*Wakara turned and tried to listen. But Great-grandmother no longer rode beside her. Instead, she saw Anne's gentle smile. "Wakara is a Yana name."*

*Then Dad's face appeared in the boiling black clouds. "Don't forget, you have Grandfather's blood too. And your mother's. Don't forget, Wakara. Don't forget your mother."*

*Lightning streaked through the clouds and set her heart thudding like the thunder. Pounding. Overpowering the sound of Lily's hooves.*

Kara gasped for breath. She sat up and threw back the sheet. It was soaked with sweat. *Awake.* The pounding should have stopped.

She heard Dad's door fly open. His footsteps rushing down the stairs. The front door squealed on its hinges and the incessant banging finally stopped.

She peered at the clock—2 A.M. Someone was at the door. It could only mean trouble.

She grabbed her robe and ran barefoot to the railing at the top of the stairs. The light in the entry hall was blazing. Dad was there. And Greg. And Sheriff Lassen.

Greg could hardly stand. He pulled away from the sheriff's grip and staggered into Dad.

"Here, let me help you get him to the couch." The sheriff grabbed the back of Greg's shirt and hauled him toward the sofa. Greg fought them, but weakly, as Dad yanked off his boots and laid him down.

98

Sheriff Lassen grunted. "Drunk and disorderly. He and that group of hooligans busted up some tables over at The Pizza Pit."

Dad looked drained. "He's a good boy, Ray. And a hard worker. He's just trying to stomp out his grief."

The sheriff nodded. "I know that, Harley. That's why I brought him home instead of throwing him in jail. When he sobers up, you tell him to do his stomping somewhere else. Next time I won't be so generous."

Greg struggled to sit up. He slouched on the sofa, his head hanging between his knees. When the sheriff left, Kara ran downstairs.

She could hardly bear the look in Dad's eyes. "Want me to make some coffee?"

"No, thanks, Wakara. I'll deal with this. You go up and check on Ryan, then get back to bed."

Kara knew he didn't mean to be harsh with her. But she also knew when her father expected to be obeyed.

Ryan was sleeping peacefully, hugging his pillow the same way she did. He had kicked the covers onto the floor. The room was warm, so Kara pulled just the sheet up over his bare feet.

When she passed the landing on her way back to bed, she could hear Greg's drunken sobbing. She peered over the banister. Dad just sat there saying nothing at all.

*Oh, God. What's happening to this family? Don't You see what a mess You caused by taking Mom away? I don't know my brother anymore.* She thought about the dream. *And now, I don't know who I am either.*

# 17

KARA GROANED AND LOOKED at the clock. "8:15. I haven't slept this late in months."

Mom would say, "Your body must have needed it." Kara heartily agreed. She would have liked to stay curled up another half hour or so, but the smell of fresh-perked coffee and frying bacon drew her out of bed.

She washed and pulled on yesterday's jeans, found a clean, sleeveless cotton shirt, then followed her nose downstairs. "Hey, what gives? I could have cooked breakfast."

Ryan was already sitting at the table chugging down a glass of orange juice. Dad was turning bacon at the stove. She had to smother a gasp of surprise when she turned and saw Greg sitting at the kitchen table.

Her brother was dressed in clean, black Wranglers, a white T-shirt, and well-polished boots. He had combed his hair, and there was a fresh razor nick on his chin. He looked sharp, except for the dark rings around his eyes. He also looked very, very sober.

"Sit down, Wakara, it's almost ready." Dad's voice was quiet. His manner calm. Yet Kara could almost feel the tension in the air.

She did as she was told. Ryan chattered his way through three pieces of bacon and a scrambled egg, then swiped his napkin across his chin and pushed back from the table. "I'm gonna watch John Wayne."

"Don't forget to rinse your plate." Kara spoke before he could bolt out of the room.

When Ryan had gone, Dad cleared his throat. "Wakara, please call Tia and tell her to be ready by two o'clock. We'll pick her up. She's not to come over beforehand."

He pulled a piece of paper out of his shirt pocket and handed it to her. "Bud Davis will be here in a few minutes to take you to town. I want you to take Ryan and pick up these supplies. You can pack when you get home. Make it around one o'clock. Greg and I have some things to do."

He looked at Greg. "You have something to say to your sister?"

Kara cringed, but Greg's voice sounded sincere when he said, "Yeah. Sorry, Wakara. I didn't mean to cause such a ruckus last night."

Dad nodded and Greg looked back down at his plate.

Kara started gathering up the dirty dishes, but Dad's hand on her arm stopped her. "Greg will do those. You just get yourself and Ryan ready, okay?"

She nodded and fled from the room. *Oh no, what's Dad going to do to Greg?* Dad had never been anything but gentle with any of them. She couldn't see him hitting Greg or anything like that, but whatever he had decided on for her brother's punishment, she was glad to be out of it.

At one o'clock they came home with the supplies and Kara sent Ryan upstairs to pack. "I'll be there in a minute."

She wandered into the kitchen. There was a note from Dad anchored with a magnet to the fridge. "Kara, I'm watering the stock. Please be ready to go by 1:45. Love, Dad."

101

She glanced at the clock. Half an hour. She grabbed two diet Cokes from the fridge and hurried up the stairs.

She had just set their duffle bags on the front porch when Dad walked up the drive from the direction of the barn. He kicked off his muddy boots and hung his work hat on one of the pegs beside the front door.

Ryan looked around. "Where's Greg? Isn't he going to say good-bye?"

Kara wanted to hug him. She hadn't dared to ask.

"Greg went with Bud Davis to check on the cattle. We'll be moving them down as soon as we close the lodge." He ruffled Ryan's hair and dropped a kiss on Kara's head. "I'll change and be right down. Ten minutes."

Mr. Davis was Dad's friend. The one who had volunteered to help out at the ranch if Greg needed him. He was also a counselor at church, and Kara suspected there was more to this trip than just checking on cattle.

Tia jabbered excitedly as they stowed their gear in the back of the tiny Cessna. But she grew quiet when Dad fired up the engine. When they lifted off, she grabbed Kara's arm and shut her eyes.

"Don't be a baby, Tia. Look, there's the river and the trail to Falcon Ridge."

But Tia refused to open her eyes or loosen her grip. Kara's arm was shooting needles by the time they landed at Eagle Lodge.

Dad lifted Ryan out, then helped Tia climb over the struts while Kara jumped to the ground. She shielded her eyes from the sun and could just see the green tractor heading toward them from behind the barn.

Kara reached up to make sure her hair was still in place. She had coiled it on top of her head this morning and pulled some tendrils free. It hadn't turned out quite as glamorous as when the stylist did it, but Tia insisted it still made her look older.

She motioned Tia over. "Colin's coming with the trailer. He'll get our bags. Come on, I'll show you around."

They met Colin at the bottom of the hill. He stopped the tractor in front of Tia. "Hi. Tia, right? Mr. Sheridan radioed you were coming. I set up a cot in Kara's room." He squinted down at Kara. "Uh, Wakara? Did you have a good time? What did you do to your hair?"

She wanted to tell him to pick his chin up off the ground, but she didn't trust her voice.

Tia answered for her. "We both got our hair done. Cool, huh?" She swished her hair down and forward, then spun around, showing off the back.

"Uh, yeah, cool. I mean, sure, it looks great. Just takes some getting used to is all." He tipped his hat and slipped into his comic drawl. "If you ladies will excuse me, I'll deliver your bags to your room."

Kara realized her hands were balled into fists and forced herself to relax. *Let him think what he wants about my hair. What does it matter?* "Come on, Tia, these jeans are hot. I want to change and check on Lily."

"Hey, slow down," Tia whispered. "He's as cute as I remembered."

Kara huffed and puffed as she climbed. *Two days away from this hill and I'm already out of shape.* "I thought you liked Devon."

Tia shrugged. "Devon's in Lariat. Colin's here. Anyway, it's not like I want to marry Colin or anything. I just said he was cute."

Kara changed into cutoffs and a T-shirt. Tia chose a new pair of white short shorts and a black, open-weaved crop top with a white sports bra underneath.

"Does your dad know you're wearing that?"

Tia shrugged, then grinned. "Pops isn't here. Mellow out, Kara. All the girls wear these."

*I'll bet.* She decided to keep it cool. "Come on. If I know Anne, she'll have a snack waiting in the dining room."

Kara wasn't disappointed. Anne had just set out a plate of oatmeal cookies and a bowl of apples. Pitchers of iced tea and lemonade were already on the serving counter.

The cook greeted Tia with a smile. "It is good to finally meet you. Wakara speaks of you often." If Anne noticed Tia's skimpy clothes, she didn't show it.

Colin noticed though. He barely said a word during dinner. Kara could tell he was trying not to stare at Tia. A couple of times she caught him looking at her hair.

After dinner, they helped Anne clean up the kitchen. Anne stored the leftover coleslaw in the fridge, then turned to Tia. "Wakara said you did well in your history class."

Tia rinsed the last of the glasses and set them in the dishwasher. "Yeah, I used to hate history, but there's some real cool stuff. We even studied about some of the Indian tribes, like back in the 1800s, you know?"

Anne smiled. "You are interested in the history of the People. Wakara has a book you might like to read. I have many others."

The generator went off at seven o'clock. By nine it was too dark to see, and Kara lit the lantern in her room. She picked up the book that Anne had given her while Tia set her things on the shelves.

"Rats. I forgot to bring a book. Where's that one Anne was talking about?"

"You mean the one her father wrote? It's right here." Kara turned the book around so Tia could see the cover.

Tia read the title out loud. "*Yana History and Folklore.* Anne's father must be pretty smart."

"I guess he was. She said he died a year or so ago. I don't know much about him." Suddenly she wished she knew more. "Anne thinks I'm part Yana instead of Nez Perce. She says Wakara is a Yana name."

"Wow. What did your dad say?"

Kara shrugged. "He said he wouldn't be surprised. There were always questions about Great-grandpa Harley's story. Dad didn't seem to care. Neither do Ryan and Greg. I guess it's all right for them. Their heritage doesn't show."

Tia scooted onto Kara's bed. "But you care, don't you?"

Kara nodded. "It's like I don't know who I am anymore. Since Mom died everything's turned upside-down. Dad says it's who I am on the inside that matters, not whether my great-grandmother was Yana or Nez Perce."

Tia sighed. "He's right, you know. You're still Wakara Windsong Sheridan, the shortest and youngest junior at Lariat High."

Kara laughed with her friend. "And you're still Tia Sanchez, the nuttiest nut case in town."

# 18

"THIS IS SO COOL, ANNE. How did your father learn all this stuff?" Tia had brought the book with her to breakfast. Now she sat at the table in the kitchen reading while Kara and Anne took a final inventory of supplies.

Anne raised her head and smiled. "The People pass down their heritage in songs and stories. My father did much research. He taught classes on Native American History. Later he rewrote his notes into books."

"Look, Kara, this says the Yana people went up and down the cliffs on ropes they made out of some weed. Ugh, no thanks. That sounds worse than flying in your dad's plane."

Anne leaned against the stove. "Many people lived in valleys like this one. They did not have airplanes to come and go. Many did not have horses either."

"So, they got in and out by ropes and vines," Kara said, pulling out a chair and sitting next to Tia. "They must have used the rocks for hand and foot holds. Like a mountain climber."

Anne nodded. "Yes. In some cases they had to carve the steps themselves."

"Like the Anasazi Indians in Mesa Verde. They built whole cities on the sides of the cliffs."

"I see you have studied well, Tia."

Tia grinned. "Pops took us to Colorado two summers ago."

Kara took a deep breath. Dad thought his grandmother's people were from the Blue Mountains. Now was a good time to see what Anne really knew. "What about in this area? Weren't there native people here too?"

"Yes. Several tribes inhabited this valley. There is evidence that they lived by the river and traveled in and out of the valley by a secret path at a place called Tunnel Falls."

Kara frowned. "I thought Pine Creek was the only trail in and out of here."

Anne sat down across from them. "I do not know. I have not seen this path. It is said to be well hidden. A precaution against invasion by an enemy."

"Well, there are lots of caves, but they aren't exactly hidden."

"The legend says, 'Where the mountains kiss, and the river drops off the edge of the world, there is a door; a pathway to the sky.'"

"That is so cool! Hey, Kara, maybe we could find it."

"Yeah, like when we have a free year or two. There's a lot more to this valley than we'll ever see. Dad hasn't even been over all of it in the Cessna."

Tia stood and stretched. "Well, I don't know about you, but all this talk about cliffs is making me dizzy. I'm going to change. Colin said we might have time to ride this afternoon."

She left the book on the table, and Kara snatched it up. For her all this talk about cliffs was confusing the issue. She might as well come out with it before Anne started on the storeroom.

"You said Wakara is a Yana name, but it can't be. Those people lived in northern California. Besides, they were extinct by the time my great-grandmother was born."

She saw a quick look of understanding cross Anne's face.

"This bothers you then. I thought it might."

Kara looked up into the familiar gentle smile.

"I do not know where your ancestor got her name. You said yourself the couple who raised her did not ask at the reservation. This is very strange. There is much mystery surrounding your heritage. Perhaps someday you will find the answers you are seeking."

"How?"

"It is like that ancient, hidden path. God knows the way, Little Moon, but only those who truly seek can find it."

*Yeah, right. Like that answers my question.* She looked down at the table so Anne couldn't see her eyes. "I guess I'd better go catch up with Tia. May I be excused?"

"Of course. The work is almost done. Enjoy your ride."

Kara nodded and escaped into the dining room before the tears she felt stinging her eyes could overflow. She swiped them away with the back of her hand and hurried down the hall. *Get a grip, Wako. You're acting like a baby.*

She almost bumped into Colin, who was just closing the door to Dad's office.

"Whoa." He gripped her arms to stop her from stumbling, then lifted her chin. "Hey, you're crying." His forehead wrinkled like an old man's. "What's wrong? Is there anything I can do?"

Somehow the compassion she saw in his eyes only made things worse. She shrugged his hands away. "It's nothing." He handed her a clean handkerchief. "Thanks." She blew her nose. "What were you doing in Dad's office?" Anything to change the subject.

108

He plucked his hat off his head, reshaped the brim, then plopped it back on. "Your dad was asking me about the youth camp I went to. He thinks it might be a good place for Greg."

"Greg?" She didn't try to hide her surprise. "Why would he want to go—Oh, you mean the camp you went to when you got in trouble." She couldn't believe it. Dad was sending Greg away.

"But isn't he a little too old for a place like that?"

Colin shrugged. "Not really. They take guys up to twenty." He started playing with his hat again. "I gave your dad the phone number." The look on his face was like Ryan's when he wasn't sure if he was in trouble or not. "We all have to deal with grief, Kara. For some of us the answers just come harder, I guess. That place helped me a lot. I think it would be good for Greg."

Before she could think of what to say, he changed the subject.

"Hey, Tia wants to ride today. I thought we could take the trail downriver, then explore that deer path Greg and I found. Remember?"

She nodded. It did sound like fun. "When?"

He looked at his watch. "Half an hour? I'll round up the horses and get the gear together."

"Hey, you two. What's all the gabbing about?" Dad stuck his head out of the office door.

Kara jumped.

He flashed a weak smile. "Sorry, Sugar Bear."

Kara forced herself to smile back. Now was not the time to question him about Greg. He looked like he'd been on a three-week cattle drive.

"We were just talking about going on a ride."

"Good. I forgot to tell you, Colin. I promised Ryan he could ride today. There's one more group coming in, then the horses go back to Lariat. He won't have many more chances before school starts."

Kara turned her head away and rolled her eyes. *Great.* What would Tia think about the pest coming along? She decided not to tell her until the last minute.

She felt a twinge of guilt. They had been excluding Ry a lot since Tia came to the lodge. Her brother didn't have anyone to play with right now. And riding Star was a treat. Maybe this would make amends.

Tia stepped out of Kara's room just as Ryan came charging down the hall. He had on a cowboy hat and riding boots, and was fumbling with a blue-and-white bandanna.

"Hey, guys, I'm ready to ride."

"Whoa, you sure are, partner." Colin took the bandanna, folded it diagonally, and tied it around Ryan's neck. "There, now you look just like John Wayne."

Ryan grinned, and Tia flashed Kara a look that said, *Is he really going?*

Kara sighed. "Okay, you guys. Give me a minute to change."

Ryan bolted for the front door. "Come on, Colin. I'll race you to the barn."

"I'd better get down there before he stampedes the entire herd." Colin tipped his hat and bowed. "Ladies. I'll see you at the barn."

Dad laughed and looked her in the eye. "Have a good time, Sugar Bear. And be careful, okay?"

She felt a rush of love for him. "We will, Dad. And don't worry. We'll be fine."

# 19

LILY WANTED TO RUN, so Kara eased her into a canter when they hit the meadow and pulled her up just short of the wooden bridge. "Sorry, girl. From here on we walk." She leaned over and patted the silky neck. No way was she going to give Colin a reason to lecture her.

They tied the horses in a ring of trees by the abandoned campsite. Ryan grabbed a stick and started poking through the cold, gray ashes in the fire ring.

"Don't make a mess, Ry." Kara opened the saddlebags and pulled out the apples and peanuts they had brought along.

Tia grabbed two small boxes of juice and carried one over to Colin, who was searching the tree line for the deer trail he and Greg had scouted in June. She handed him the juice. "Here, Col, I thought you might be thirsty. Hey, are you sure there's a trail here? It looks pretty bushy. Isn't that, like, poison oak?"

Kara had an instant picture of Tia covered head to toe in an itchy red rash. She knew she should be ashamed of herself, but the image made her smile. Tia turned calf-eyed every time she was anywhere near Colin. Not that she should

111

care—Tia flirted with all the guys—but for some reason Kara felt betrayed when her best friend acted like that with Colin.

"Wow!" Ryan dropped to his knees and began digging through the ashes with his hands. "Way cool! Look, Colin, real bullets."

Kara grabbed Ryan's arm, then relaxed when he held out a handful of empty copper-tipped cartridges. "Throw those things back," she ordered. "They're filthy. And you'd better put your shirt back on. You'll get a sunburn."

Ryan glared at her then turned away, stuffing the spent bullets into the pocket of his jeans. He snatched something else out of the ashes and ran to stuff it in the leather pouch hanging from Star's saddle.

Kara sighed as she watched him carefully tie his long-sleeved shirt around his waist, leaving his back bare. She knew she should make him obey her, but maybe a sunburn would teach him a lesson.

Tia hollered, "Hey, you guys, let's get with it. Colin found the trail." Her face was flushed, and she didn't look a bit worried about poison oak.

Colin had been right. It was only a deer track, dusty and so narrow in places that they had to turn sideways to push through the thorny brush.

They walked single file with Colin in the lead, then Tia and Ryan, with Kara bringing up the rear. Colin stopped with a finger to his lips and pointed out deer feeding on the dry, brown grasses just inside the tree line.

Kara felt sorry for the animals. They looked skinny and weak. Even the fir trees were turning brown in this heat.

Tia screamed and the deer scattered.

Kara pushed past Ryan. "What is it?"

Colin was already hovering, working something out of Tia's hair. "It's just a twig. See? Good thing your hair is short. It pulled right out."

Tia flushed. "Sorry. Something grabbed me. I didn't know what it was."

Ryan wiggled between them. "Let me see. Aw, I thought it was a snake or something." He sounded so disappointed, even Tia had to laugh.

Colin turned and started down the trail. Kara fell back to her spot behind Ryan. His arms were getting scratched, and his back was already turning red. She should make him put his shirt on, but it wasn't worth the fight.

"It must be 95 degrees in here." Colin took a swig of water from his canteen.

Kara drank, then handed the canteen to Ryan. "It looks like it opens up ahead." She pointed to where the trail topped a small rise, then seemed to end in a halo of light.

Colin followed her gaze. "Man, I hope so. I could use some fresh air." He looked at his pedometer and let out a low whistle. "I can't believe it, but we've come three miles already."

Kara grimaced. She could believe it. Her feet were throbbing inside her hiking boots, her hair felt sticky and heavy on top of her head. Sometimes she wished she had gotten it cut like Tia's. A hundred yards ahead the trail ended in a small clearing. Boulders the size of a small house shot up in front of them. The forest closed in thickly to the right, and on their left the ground dropped off twenty feet or more into the river below.

Tia sat down and pulled off her tennis shoes. "Ow! Look at the blisters." She propped herself against a tree and stretched, peering through one eye at Colin. "I am totally done. Someone will just have to carry me back."

*In your dreams.* Kara bit back the retort and said instead, "I told you to wear hiking boots."

Tia shrugged. "They're too stiff. I'd have blisters all the way up to my ankles."

113

Colin broke into their conversation. "Listen."

When they stopped talking, they could hear the sound of water rushing over rocks.

Colin slipped off his backpack and handed it to Kara. "The river's too shallow to make that much noise. There must be a waterfall. I'm going to climb over and have a look."

Colin was halfway up the pile of boulders when Ryan called out, "Hey, look, you guys. You can see it from here!"

Kara gasped. He was standing on tiptoes at the edge of the canyon, pointing eagerly to where the water flowed through a huge hole in the rock face. "Ryan Sheridan, come away from there!"

He scowled at her. "I'm not doin' nothing, I just want to see." He took another step, then his arms flailed wildly as the ground crumbled beneath his feet. Before Kara could move, he landed hard on his bottom, then slid with an avalanche of rocks and dirt over the edge.

Everything seemed to happen in slow motion. Kara could hear Tia's frantic screams. She heard Colin yell, "Hang on, I'm coming!" Then she was at the spot where her little brother had disappeared.

She grabbed a low-hanging tree branch, leaned out, and scanned the river below. The water flowed shallow and clear. There was no sign of a body, only rocks. Her eyes darted back up over the face of the cliff.

Tia was still screaming, "Oh, no! Ryan! Oh, no!"

Kara's patience snapped. "Tia, shut up! I have to listen for Ry."

The tree branch was slippery in her sweaty hand. She got a better grip and leaned even farther out over the edge.

Then she spotted him. He sat, hugging his knees to his chest, on a small ledge only a few feet from the top of the cliff. He had scooted back as far as he could under the overhanging rock. She could just see the front of his body.

114

"Don't you move, Ry! Not even a wiggle, do you hear me?"

He buried his face between his knees.

She took a deep breath. *Stay calm. Think it through.* The only rope she had was three miles away, hanging from Lily's saddle. Anyway, the ledge was too small to lower anyone down. And the lodge was too far away to go for help. He could panic any minute and tumble into the river.

A whimper from the huddled form spurred her into action. She threw herself on the ground and scooted toward the edge. "Tia. Grab my ankles!"

"I can't! Kara, don't, you'll fall!"

"I've got you. Go slow." Kara felt Colin's strong hands grip her ankles as she eased her way over the ledge.

*Don't look down. Focus on Ryan.* She took a deep breath, then scooted forward. Another few inches and she'd be all the way over, and Colin might not be able to hold her. "Ryan. Look at me."

He shuddered, but he didn't raise his head.

"Ry, come on, I can't quite reach. You have to help."

Colin spoke from behind her. "Come on, partner. It's getting late. We gotta get back and feed that horse of yours. You wouldn't want Star to go hungry, would you?"

Ryan looked up, and the terror on his face made Kara's heart pound. She forced herself to smile. "Hi," she said gently. "Scoot out just a little and lift your arms so I can reach you, okay?"

He didn't move.

Kara took a deep breath. *Please, God, make him listen.* She tried again. "Ryan, grab my arms. I won't let you fall, I promise. Colin won't let either of us fall; he's going to pull us up, just like in that John Wayne movie. Remember?"

His arms inched upward. She could touch his hands, but she couldn't get a grip. He was too far under the overhang.

He would have to slide forward and turn around. If she tried to bring him up the way he was, he could break his back.

She could hear Tia sobbing. Then Colin's rough voice, "If you can't help, be quiet or go away!"

Sweat dripped from her forehead. She wiped her slippery hands on the dusty rocks and tried to ignore the pain in her legs and thighs. "A little farther, Ry. Come on."

"Come on, partner, you can do it." Colin's voice was close and comforting. She felt his grip tighten around her lower legs.

Suddenly Ryan moved forward. Eyes squeezed shut, his arms shot high above his head. Kara grabbed his forearms and felt his slender fingers wrap around her wrists.

"I've got you. Now stand up."

He let her pull him to his feet. Kara let her breath out, then filled her lungs again, muscles taut. "Turn around, Ry, you have to face the rocks."

She shifted her grip as he obeyed. *Okay. We have to do this in a hurry.* Up and out in one smooth motion.

"Let's get out of here, Ry. Use your legs if you can."

He nodded.

"Okay. One, two, three."

Colin started to pull her backward.

Then Kara's hands slipped. For a split second she thought she had lost him. Ryan's legs pumped air, then connected with the rock face as he helped propel himself up the cliff.

When she was all the way back on solid ground, Colin released her, grabbed the back of Ryan's jeans, and lifted him up over the edge.

116

# 20

"OH, RY. YOU SCARED US all to death." Kara held him until they both stopped shaking. "Do you hurt anywhere?"

"His back." Colin's face looked grim.

She quickly turned Ryan around. His bare back was scraped and bloody, pitted with rocks and dirt.

Colin unfolded his bandanna. "Here, use this. The inside's clean. I'll get some water."

Ryan winced as she gently washed the wounds, but he didn't cry.

"That's the best I can do. Here, soak his shirt, the damp will at least cool his sunburn." Colin emptied the third canteen on Ryan's shirt, then helped her ease it over his shoulders.

Somehow they made it back down the trail. She and Colin took turns carrying Ryan when he couldn't walk any farther. When they reached the horses, Colin lifted him gently to the front of Kara's saddle.

"There you go, Tiger. I'll lead Star, okay?"

"I want to ride him."

It was the first he had spoken since they'd pulled him up the cliff. Kara laughed, relieved. "No way, Jose. You stick with me until we get home."

117

She knew it was getting late, but she forced herself to keep to a walk. Anything faster would be painful for Ry.

She wasn't surprised to find Dad at the barn saddling a horse to search for them. The look of relief on his face when they rode in made her want to cry.

Ryan did cry then as Dad lifted him from her saddle.

"It's his back, Mr. Sheridan," Tia sobbed. "He fell off the cliff. It wasn't anybody's fault."

*Way to go, Tia.* Kara glared at her. "He's pretty scratched up, Dad, but nothing's broken."

"Is everybody else okay?"

Kara nodded.

Colin squeezed her shoulder, then took Lily's reins. "You guys go on up. I'll take care of the horses."

Dad laid Ryan gently on his bed. Anne took one look at Ryan's shredded back and hustled into the kitchen. She returned with one of the plants she kept on the windowsill. "Aloe." She slit open several of the leaves and applied the sticky substance to Ryan's wounds. "By tomorrow his skin will begin to heal."

Later, Anne took in a bowl of chicken soup and some herbal tea. Ryan polished it off like he hadn't eaten in a week. The next time Kara peeked in, she found him curled up sleeping like a puppy on a rug.

Kara and Tia turned in early too, but Kara's sheet felt like a lead weight pinning her to the bed. Every time she closed her eyes, Ryan's terrified face flashed into her mind. She finally gave up trying to sleep.

Tia snored softly from her cot just a few feet away. Kara bit her lip to keep from crying out as her leg muscles cramped. Her arms felt like taut rubber bands, and her abdomen burned from being pulled along the ground. But she was nowhere near as sore as Ryan. Between the sunburn

118

and the cuts and scratches, his back looked like a piece of raw meat.

She couldn't stay cooped up in here. She needed fresh air and a place to be alone. When the leg cramps passed, she tiptoed past Tia, pulled on her jeans, and eased open the bedroom door. Once in the hallway, she switched on her flashlight. In two minutes she was out the door and into the night.

The air was still warm, and insects hummed in the dry, brown grass. Something slithered past her foot, and she began to wish she'd worn tennis shoes instead of thongs. If she went back she'd wake Tia. Then she'd have to explain what she was doing up at this time of night.

*No. Not this time.* She didn't want to talk about it anymore. Explaining to Dad had been hard enough. Not that he blamed her. Anne didn't either. Colin had told them how she hadn't even hesitated going over the cliff after Ryan. But she still felt like it was her fault. She wasn't watching him closely enough.

She hadn't been very nice to him lately either. And today, when she needed him to listen, he wouldn't budge. Not until Colin talked to him. It was Colin he trusted, not her.

Her eyes burned. She couldn't cry; she had to think. She followed the well-worn path through the trees to the spot where a huge, flat rock overlooked the river. It was a popular spot with the guests who liked to fish or broil their bodies in the afternoon sun. But at night, and in the very early morning, it was a private place where she could think or dream.

Anne used it as a place to pray. She'd seen Anne in the evenings standing on the deck and staring into space, her expression empty yet somehow filled with peace.

*I wish I could do that.* Dad and Mom had told her God was always there. If that was true, why couldn't she find Him?

She tried to concentrate on the ripple of water in the river and the dry, dusty smell of rocks and earth. But her thoughts refused to change focus. *God never changes.*

*If He never changes, then He's always there.*

*But if He's always there, it must be me who's run away.*

She didn't even bother to wipe the tears off her cheeks. Everything was her fault. She was responsible for the distance between herself and God. She fought Anne's attempts to be her friend. She was surly with Ryan.

Her thoughts tumbled on. *I'm more worried about where my name came from than I am about taking care of my little brother.*

*Self-pity doesn't cut it, Wakara. Let go and get a grip on God.*

"Oh, great. Now Colin's in on it." But she knew the voice in her head was right.

"I've been trying to do it all myself, haven't I, God?" She could barely hear her own whisper, but she knew He could hear. "I've been so busy blaming everybody else for my pain. I've been so mad at You, I haven't even let You help me."

What was it Anne had said? "There is a wild fire raging in your heart, Little Moon. Anger burns you up inside. But God's Spirit is a cleansing fire. If you let Him, He will purify your soul."

She wrapped her arms around her knees and hugged them to her chest. The stars flashed bright in the clear, dark sky. They looked close enough to touch. Mom was out there. In heaven. Out beyond the stars. "I want her here with me," Kara prayed, "but if she can't be, will You please come instead? I need You. I can't do this alone."

The night settled around her like a warm, dark quilt. She felt a strange sort of comfort in the rustling of leaves, the trickling of water over rock. A breeze fanned the hair along her cheeks. She brushed the tickling sensation away and inhaled the warm, pine-scented air.

*My peace I give to you . . . do not let your heart be troubled and do not be afraid.* The Scripture came back to her, vivid and fresh as if she'd memorized it yesterday. And she felt the warmth of God's love, like a fire in her heart.

▲

When Kara got back to her room, Tia was sitting upright on her cot, searching the room with her flashlight.

"Tia?" Kara closed the door behind her and kept her voice low. "What are you doing?"

"Looking for my shoes," Tia whispered. "Where have you been? I was coming to find you. I wanted to make sure you were okay and tell you I'm going home. Your dad can fly me out in the morning when he takes Ryan to the doctor."

Kara frowned and sat on the end of the cot. "Why?"

"You gotta be kidding! I really screwed up, didn't I? Blubbering all over the place. I'm no good in an emergency. All I do is get in the way and make everybody mad. Besides, this place is too dangerous for me. You and Colin can handle it. I can't. End of story."

Kara didn't know what to say. Tia was right. She had been in the way during the rescue.

"He likes you, you know. I wasn't really trying to take him away, just having some fun," Tia said miserably.

"What are you talking about?"

"Don't be a stupe. Anyone with half a brain can see Colin's interested in you." She pulled her legs up, wrapped her arms around them, and lowered her chin to her knees. "I'm sorry I ruined our week."

"Now who's being a stupe?" An hour ago Kara had been thinking the same thing. But it really hadn't been all Tia's fault.

"Look, I'm the one who's sorry. I haven't been a very good friend lately." Tia was staring at her, so she hurried

121

on. "And anyway, Colin isn't interested in either of us. He's Greg's age. We're just kids to him."

"Right. If you believe that, you're worse than a stupe; you're blind."

Kara yawned. "Okay, okay. But can't we talk about it in the morning?" She suddenly felt like she'd wrestled a grizzly. She ached all over, and her cuts and bruises stung. She was so tired she couldn't think past morning, yet she felt a quietness inside that hadn't been there in a long, long time.

This time when she slipped into her bed, she fell instantly asleep.

# 21

KARA BLINKED AT THE BRIGHT sunlight flooding through the window. The whine of an airplane engine drew her out of bed just as the door opened and Tia crept into the room.

Kara rubbed her eyes. "Wow, I must have really slept. What's going on? Is that Mark with the new guests?" She grabbed for her jeans. "Rats, they're supposed to go in cabin one and it's not even clean yet."

Tia laughed. "Will you relax? Anne and I cleaned the cabin, but those people aren't coming. Mark called on the radio. The guests canceled, so he's flying in Doctor Glenn instead."

She stopped and took a deep breath. "That means your dad's not flying out, so you'll like have to put up with me until Mark leaves."

"Oh, Tia." Kara wrapped her friend in a hug. "What would I do without you? Please don't go. Wait until the end of the week."

"You mean that?" Tia's face crumbled. Kara was relieved when she sniffed and smiled. "Cool. I'll stay, as long as you promise not to work me to death."

"It's a promise. You can sit and watch Anne and me get ready to close the place. We won't even try to make you feel guilty." She grinned and shrugged into a clean cotton shirt. "Come on. The plane's landed and I want to hear what the doctor has to say about Ryan."

She ran a comb through her hair, swiped at her teeth with the toothbrush, and hurried out onto the front deck. Dad and Doc Glenn were heading up the hill with Mark and two other men trailing behind.

She shielded her eyes and stared. "Greg?"

Tia was right behind her. "Oh yeah, I forgot. Greg came with. When those people canceled, your dad decided to close the lodge early. Greg and Mr. Davis are supposed to take the horses out."

"Boy, that'll teach me to sleep late." She grinned at Tia. "Is there anything else I should know about?"

"Well, Anne said if you want any bacon or juice you'd better grab it before the men get here. Ryan's already had his share and more."

Kara grabbed a glass of juice and a bagel, and followed the men into Ryan's room. Ry was lying on his stomach with his head and arms hanging over the edge of the bed, playing with a couple of plastic cowboy figures.

The doctor ordered everybody but Dad out of the room. Kara and Tia had to jump back when the door opened again. Both Dad and Doc were smiling.

"He'll be fine in a day or two. Wounds are nice and clean. Your cook did a good job with the aloe vera. The tetanus shot and these antibiotics should take care of the rest."

Doc stowed his medical kit in the back of Mark's plane and pulled out his fishing rod. "Since I'm here, I might as well take back a souvenir."

When Doc and Mark had disappeared upriver, Dad called a family meeting. "Looks like we close up a week early. Kara, you and Tia help Anne get the cabins in shape. I'd like Colin to see if he can shore up that barn.

"Greg and Bud will take the horses out on Friday. We'll leave Lily and Dakota here just in case. Colin can ride out when everything's done. Agreed?"

"I can ride Lily out, Dad." Kara tensed, expecting him to say no, but he surprised her.

"Let's wait and see, Sugar Bear. It depends on what needs doing at home."

In spite of her teasing that they were working her to death, Tia pitched in and helped with the chores. The cabins were stripped of linens, floors scrubbed, windows scaled tight. By Friday afternoon, the only things left to clean were the bedrooms in the lodge.

Kara woke up at 5 A.M. on Saturday with an uneasy feeling in the pit of her stomach. She had dreamed about Mom again last night. Not the usual nightmare about running through the fire. This time she was back at the grave site, saying a final good-bye.

The dream faded, but her cheeks stayed damp with tears. *August 28. Tomorrow it will have been a year.* Bad enough, but Dad had an appointment in Lariat and was flying Tia out today. She wished he wouldn't go.

"You and Ry stay and help Colin and Anne finish up," he had said. But when she asked why he couldn't just take Ryan with him, he hadn't given her an answer. Not a good one anyway.

"Ryan's back is still sore. I want him to rest another day or two." He kissed her brow. "Don't worry, Sugar Bear, I'll be back to get Ryan and Anne Monday morning. If the weather holds, you can ride out with Colin. Greg will be waiting at the trailhead with a trailer."

The thought struck her, *Maybe Dad wants to be alone.* She sighed and swung her legs over the edge of the bed. Dad had said he wanted to get an early start. It was time to wake Tia.

▲

Kara hooked her thumbs over the front pockets of her jeans and watched Dad load Tia's bag into the Cessna. "Thanks for all the help, Tia. I'm really glad you got to come," she said.

"Yeah. I guess it all turned out okay." Tia sighed. "Anyway, two weeks and it's back to the school zone." Her face brightened. "Hey, when you get home we'll have to hit the sales!"

Dad was motioning Tia to come. "Gotta go. See you in a few."

Dad had one foot on the wing, ready to hoist himself into the cockpit. Kara was about to turn away when he stepped down and walked back to her. His brow wrinkled as he squinted against the glaring sun.

"Mark says there's another fire burning over behind Falcon Ridge. I'm sure it won't get this far, but everything's so dry. Remember, no campfire or barbecue, okay?"

"Don't worry, Dad, we'll be fine."

She shielded her eyes to watch the plane take off. When it disappeared behind a ridge of Ponderosa pines, she swung her gaze to the right and noticed thunderheads building over Cedar Butte.

Back at the lodge she found Anne in the kitchen packing up her fishing gear.

"There are still fish at Otter Lake. I will bring some for our dinner." She hoisted the gear onto a backpack and started for the door.

"Why the backpack?"

"Colin is checking the fence line. He has Dakota. I will walk."

Kara felt the flush spread up her neck and blossom into two hot patches on her cheeks. She took a deep breath. How could she have been so selfish before? "Please take Lily."

126

Anne turned and smiled at her gently. "Are you sure?"

"Yes." She felt that strange sense of quiet inside, like she'd felt the other night. "I really want you to."

When Anne left, Kara peeked in on Ryan. He had fallen asleep on his stomach, arms dangling over the edge of the bed, a comic book spread across the throw rug on the floor.

She decided not to wake him. She'd leave his room 'til last. It would take a couple of hours to do her own.

By 10 A.M. her shelves were empty, and everything was free of dust. She stuffed her sheets and bedspread into a plastic bag and spread her sleeping bag on top of the mattress cover. Two more nights. Everything was packed except for the necessities.

When she checked on Ryan, he wasn't in his room. She heard his voice coming from the kitchen. "Dad? Hey, Dad, you there?"

The radio.

She hurried through the kitchen. Sure enough, he was in the radio room fiddling with the buttons and dials. She started to yell, then changed her tone. "Ry, Dad's probably not there. He had to take Tia home, remember?"

Ryan jumped, and the hand mike went flying. She grabbed for it, but too late. The instrument crashed to the floor, breaking open the casing and exposing the wiring inside.

She gasped. "Oh, no!" Ryan looked at her, then burst into tears. She wanted to cry herself. That radio had cost a fortune. Dad was going to have a fit. She bent to pick up the debris and realized her hands were shaking like she'd had three cups of coffee this morning instead of one.

She tried to keep her voice steady. "This is why you're not supposed to be in here." His face flooded with fear, and she relented. "Maybe Colin can fix it." *Let's just hope we don't need it between now and then.*

# 22

KARA DUSTED DAD'S AND RYAN'S room while her brother packed his duffle bag for the trip home. At noon, she left him fiddling with a small canvas pouch he'd found in the barn. He called it his "survival kit," and he had been storing treasures in it all summer.

"Anne should be home any minute. I'll see what we have . . ."

A rumble of thunder drowned out her words. The front door crashed open. Colin rushed into the lodge and leaned against the door until it closed against the howling wind.

"Whoa. That's gonna be some storm. I moved Dakota to an outside stall. The barn's not all that stable." He stripped off his work gloves and tossed his hat onto the rack by the door. "I was going to put Lily out there too, but I see Anne's not back."

Lightning flashed. The lights stayed on. Kara said a silent prayer of thanks for the generator. But she was worried about Anne. "She should have been back by now."

She flinched as another peal of thunder rocked the lodge. A gale-driven rain began pounding the deck, turning the huge windows into sheets of streaming water.

Colin had to yell to make himself heard. "Anne's smart. She probably saw the storm coming and took cover."

Kara nodded, but she felt uneasy. *I just hope he's right.*

She found a can of tuna, grabbed the mayonnaise from the fridge, and mixed the filling for sandwiches. Her stomach felt too jumpy to eat, but Colin and Ryan gobbled down two apiece. Ryan had just headed for his room when she noticed the quiet.

"Storm's over." Colin looked at his watch. "We'll give Anne another half hour. If she's not back by then, I'll go look for her."

Kara shivered. In just the last few days she'd begun to realize how much Anne meant to her. The cook had shown her nothing but kindness—even when she acted like a jerk. What if something had happened to her? What if she had been hit by lightning? Or maybe Lily had spooked and thrown her.

But Lily never spooked. At least not from thunder. Besides, if Lily were loose, she would have headed home. Her thoughts spun like a child's windup toy. An intense ache began to spread up the back of her head.

"Colin?"

"I know." He was standing right behind her. His fingers began to knead her shoulders, and she felt the muscles start to relax. "I'm worried too. But let's give her some time, okay?"

The front door slammed again. She jumped up and followed Colin into the dining room. But it was only Ryan standing outside on the deck.

"Hey, wow, you guys gotta see this."

The entire yard was strewn with pine branches and shreds of bark. Two trees had come crashing down inches from the lodge. Dad had always been careful to keep thirty feet of clearing between the buildings and the woods. It was sup-

129

posed to be for fire safety, but now Kara realized there was more than one reason for the rule. Those two trees could have easily taken out the roof.

She switched her gaze toward the barn and gasped. One whole side had caved in, leaving a huge pile of wood slats and tree branches where the stalls should have been.

"Oh, Colin. Thank God you kept Dakota outside."

Colin jumped off the deck and sprinted toward the corral. "Keep Ryan here," he yelled over his shoulder. "It might not be safe."

But she couldn't just stand there. What if Lily had come home? What if Anne had headed for the barn and gotten trapped? She started to order Ryan to stay, but she knew that would never happen. "Come on, Ry. But stay away from the barn. I mean it."

Breathless, she caught up with Colin just as he was leading Dakota from one of the outside stalls. They had been built against the back of the plane hangar so the string horses could have shelter from the sun or rain. Most were open in the front, like an up-ended cardboard box. But two had been built with doors for isolating animals. They were new, solid, and safe.

"Not a scratch. He's antsy, but not hurt."

Kara sighed in relief. "Should we check the barn?"

Colin threw a saddle blanket over Dakota's back. "Not now. I'm going after Anne."

She could hear the anxiety in his voice and followed his gaze. A plume of thick, white smoke was rising from behind the mountains to the north. *Forest fire.* She watched, mesmerized, as the sky took on a reddish glow, then darkened as the smoke began to spread.

"It's miles away." Colin's voice jerked her out of her daze. He held Dakota's reins in one hand and slipped his other arm around her shoulders, giving her a gentle squeeze. "I'll find her, Wakara." He vaulted into the saddle. "Get on the radio. Get Mark or your dad back in here. We might need the plane."

Dakota danced sideways. Colin spun him around to face her. "If that fire gets any closer and I'm not back, you're out of here. Got it?"

"No way. I won't leave you . . . Colin!" But he had pushed Dakota to a full gallop. In seconds they were out of sight.

She felt Ryan's hand slip into hers. "Kara? Is the fire gonna come here?" His forehead was creased with worry as he stared wide-eyed at the rapidly darkening sky.

She ruffled his hair. With an effort she kept her voice light. "I don't think so. Colin will find Anne, then Dad will come and take us home." Even as she said it, she remembered the broken radio mike and felt the first wild rush of fear.

After an hour she gave up trying to fix the radio. She picked up the binoculars and scanned the mountains one more time. Smoke had spread like a huge, dark quilt across the sky. In the far north, the reddish glow leaped into great orange flames, devouring the landscape like a giant tongue, lapping up everything ahead of it.

Colin and Anne were nowhere in sight.

Ryan pressed his nose against the window. "It's getting closer, isn't it?"

She didn't try to lie. "Yes." She took a deep breath. They couldn't just sit here and wait. The flames were heading southeast along Cedar Butte. If the fire jumped the ridge, it'd be headed right for Otter Lake.

"Get your pack, Ryan, and your canteen. Extra socks and shoes, okay? And your jacket too."

"But it's hot."

"This is no time to argue. Just do it, Ry. Please."

He bolted for his room.

131

She stuffed her compass, extra clothes, her jacket, binoculars, and a small first aid kit into her pack, then filled both canteens and two plastic bottles with water. Ryan stood still while she shoved two apples and a couple packs of raisins into his backpack.

"All set?" She tried to stay calm, but her hands were shaking and her throat felt like sandpaper.

"I'm scared."

She turned him around and pulled him in for a hug. "So am I, Kiddo. That's why we have to get out of here. We'll find the others and go out through Pine Creek."

If the fire hadn't already spread that far.

# 23

ASHES DRIFTED LIKE SOOTY snowflakes from the sky. A great plume of smoke spread across the valley, causing Kara's breath to come in gasps as she jogged down the hill. Suddenly, she slowed down, realizing that Ryan probably couldn't keep up. Forcing herself to a fast walk, she turned her head and saw him trotting just behind her. So far, so good.

At the bottom of the hill, she picked up the pace again. Past the empty corral, past the ruined barn. What if Lily and Dakota had been in there? She didn't even want to think about that.

She turned right at the empty hangar where Dad's plane had been parked just a few hours ago. Would he come back to get them? What if he did, and they weren't there? She should have left a note, but she had been in too much of a hurry. He would understand. Anne, or even Colin, might be injured.

She paused at the edge of the runway. The stiff, brown grass was pocked by small round holes. Prairie dogs. Colin called them whistle pigs. On a normal day there would be hundreds of them perched at the entrance to their dens, barking their shrill warning. But today there wasn't any sign of the small, querulous creatures.

Come to think of it, they weren't out this morning either when she had come to see Dad off. They were hiding in their dens. They must have known.

*Dad should have known. He shouldn't have left us.*

She knew that wasn't fair. If he had thought there was any danger, he wouldn't have gone.

"My bag!"

She spun around. "Ryan? Wait!"

But he was already running back toward the lodge. "I forgot my survival kit. We might need it."

"Ryan, no!" But either he didn't hear her or was deliberately ignoring her screams. She started after him, then stopped. Better to save her energy. He'd be back before she could get up the hill.

A steady rumbling, like thunder, interrupted her thoughts. The ground began to shake. Now what? She grabbed hold of the fence post to keep her balance. Elk! A herd of at least a hundred of them stampeded toward the river. Moving at breakneck speed, they kicked up rocks and mowed down small trees like matchsticks.

If she and Ryan had been on the runway they'd have been trampled. She watched the herd disappear around the curve of the river, then swung her head around to see where they had come from.

Bald Mountain. The dust from the panicked animals, added to the smoke, made her eyes water even more. But she didn't need the binoculars to see the yellow-orange flames leaping from one tree to the next on the highest ridge.

Ten miles away. Fifteen tops. What would happen when the fire reached the river? There wasn't enough water. Nothing would stop it.

She felt a rush of panic. Where was that kid? Then she saw him running down the hill. "Come on, Ryan!" she shouted over the lump in her throat. "We need to move." Fire burned more slowly downhill, she consoled herself. They had time. They had to have time.

A thin layer of ashes made the ground slippery. Ryan slid the last few feet into her leg and nearly knocked her off her feet. "Whew. I got it. It was right on the table—Wow! Look at that!"

The awe in his voice turned to fear. "It's coming this way."

Not if they went downstream. But by going toward Otter Lake they were headed right toward the fire. Still she had to find Colin and Anne. They didn't have much time. How could she get Ryan to understand without scaring him to death?

She forced herself to stay calm. It wouldn't help to yell at him. Yelling would just make him angry, then he wouldn't listen at all. She took hold of his shoulders and turned him to face her. "Ry, look at me."

To her surprise, he obeyed. His eyes were wide, his lower lip quivering. "Ryan, you have to stay with me from now on, okay? It's important. You have to listen and do what I say."

He nodded and took hold of her hand. "Are we going to find Anne now?"

"We're going to try."

She found the faint line of bare dirt where the horses had crossed the meadow. The fire was moving parallel to them, southeast along the ridge. Had it already jumped the gorge to their side? She couldn't tell.

She ducked her head. The wind was driving the heat and smoke right at them. Her face was beginning to burn. She moved quickly, careful to keep herself between Ryan and the worst of it. The air was thick with the scorched-earth smell of burning brush.

A blizzard of ashes mixed with bark and pine needles rained from the sky. Ryan stumbled, then stopped and rubbed at his eyes. "My eyes hurt, Kara, and I can't breathe. I want to go back."

Her own eyes were watering so much she could hardly see. She had to fight the urge to turn and run the other way. What if they didn't find Anne and Colin? Once they made Otter Lake, there would be no more choices. The only way out was the steep, switchback trail to Pine Creek.

"Here, grab on to my backpack. We're almost to the trail."

Three mule deer, a buck and two does, rushed past heading west, away from the flames. Ryan's feet dragged. Kara urged him on. "Look, Ry. There's the path." She steered him to the right and turned away from the fire. The heat was to her back now, so she pushed him in front of her. "A few more feet and we'll stop to rest."

*Pop. Crash.* The sky exploded into a ball of light. She pushed Ryan to the ground and fell across him, covering her head. For a heartbeat it was quiet. Nothing moved. She raised her head and saw flames licking hungrily at the brittle needles of a fallen fir tree.

A hot wind blew across her cheek. She squeezed her eyes shut and pressed her hands to her ears. That sound. That horrible, screeching, roaring sound. Like a freight train hurtling through the trees.

It was the same as in her dream. Mom was calling her. *Wakara, run.* The voice seemed to be coming from the flames. *Knock it off. The voice isn't real.* She tried to take a deep breath, but her lungs felt like they were going to explode.

Pinpricks of fire seared her bare arms and brought her up on her knees. She could smell burning cloth and hair. They were on fire! She knocked one large ember off Ryan's collar and brushed wildly at her hair.

136

Ryan coughed and sat up, his breath making whooshing sounds next to her ear. She grabbed his backpack, hauled him up, and ran, half dragging him back down the trail, toward the lodge. Kara hated to give up their search for Colin and Anne already, but she knew they could never make it to Otter Lake in this heat and smoke. She realized they were in serious danger even heading away from the fire now. Now, they had to make it to the river.

When they reached the meadow, she picked Ryan up and began to run blindly. Her lungs burned. She forced her legs to move faster. Then her foot caught the edge of a hole. She stumbled forward, lost her grip on Ryan, and hit the ground.

She lay still, trying not to cry, trying even harder to catch her breath. *Stupid prairie dogs!* Ryan had rolled away from her. She could hear him coughing a few feet away. She tried to call out to him, but her tongue felt thick, as if it was glued to the roof of her mouth.

They weren't going to make it. She felt a fresh rush of fear. *Oh, God, if You don't help us we're going to die.*

Was this how Mom had felt when she was trapped in the flames? *No. Mom had been unconscious. She couldn't have known.* Kara felt a quiet settle over her. She could almost feel her mother's cool hands brushing the heat from her face.

She cupped her hands and put them over her mouth, filtering the smoky air. When her heartbeat slowed, she moved each arm and then her legs. Everything worked.

She rolled to her knees. The fall had torn holes in her jeans. Her hands and both knees were bleeding. She pushed to her feet, brushing at the dirt and pebbles imbedded like a thousand needles in her skin.

Ryan was crawling toward her, a dull, faraway look in his eyes.

*No. Not now.* He couldn't lose it now. There was no way she could carry him any farther.

"Ry." She lifted him to his feet. "It's okay, Ryan. It's going to be okay." She winced as his arms clamped around her waist. He clung to her like a lifeline.

She held him a second longer, then gently pried him away. "Do you hurt anywhere?" He held out his hands. They were scraped like hers, and a small cut decorated his forehead above one eye.

She realized the heat had lessened, yet the smoke was just as thick. "We have to follow the river now. It's our only way out. Can you be brave and help me?"

He nodded, and she felt a stab of hope. "God will take care of us."

Somehow, saying the words out loud, she knew it was true.

# 24

THE MINAM RIVER WAS CLOSER than she had thought. But the raging white water that had rushed and whirled across the rocks last spring had shrunk to a narrow, shallow stream.

Black cinders popped and hissed in the water, but still it felt like heaven. She lay down flat in it and told Ryan to do the same. "Soak yourself. But don't drink it. Here." She pulled the canteen from the side of her pack and handed it to him. "Not too much, it might have to last awhile."

She swallowed a mouthful of water, then untied Ryan's bandanna from around his neck and soaked it in the river. "Here, tie this around your nose and mouth."

His eyes lit up. "Like a bandit."

She laughed, then choked and swallowed against the burning in her throat. They needed to move. But the water felt so good.

"Kara?" Ryan was holding something out to her.

"What's this?"

"Buerscosh." He already had his tongue wrapped around a piece of hard candy.

"Butterscotch? Thanks!" The moist candy tasted like honey and soothed her burning throat. "What else have you got in there?"

But he had already tightened the drawstring on his "survival kit" and refused to open it.

Six loud pops like firecrackers sent her scrambling to her feet as a fresh deluge of cinders fell around them into the water. She turned and watched in horror as a great orange wall of flame shot into the air at a curve upriver and began to leap from tree to tree. "Oh, no! A crown fire!" It was still moving the other way, but the wind could blow burning leaves and branches for miles. "Let's get out of here."

She started to run, but the acrid, black smoke seared her lungs. She dropped to the water. "Hands and knees, Ry. You can breathe easier close to the ground." She bit her lip to keep from crying out as rocks and pebbles cut into her already stinging skin.

She crawled fast, pushing Ryan along in front of her, but he moved clumsily. She felt the familiar chest-squeezing fear. This time the nightmare was real.

The riverbed dropped and curved. She surged forward. "Faster, Ryan, come on, we have to move."

"I can't!" His voice caught on a sob.

He was exhausted. So was she. And so thirsty she could drink the river dry.

Ryan slipped and fell flat. She let herself drop beside him into the shallow water and willed herself not to panic. The banks now sloped a good five feet above them. Down here the air was not as thick. It would be easier to walk instead of crawl, and they would still be able to breathe.

Clouds of smoke hovered to the north and east. Bursts of flame shot sparks into the sky like fireworks on the Fourth of July.

Her hands were numb. She used her teeth to open the canteen and handed it to Ryan. "Drink."

He chugged down half the container before she grabbed it away. A tingling pain rushed up her arms as she guzzled the rest. Her throat still burned. They had two bottles and the other canteen.

It would have to be enough.

"Yuck!" Ryan gagged as a dead trout floated by, belly-up. Another followed, then another. She pulled him to his feet.

Ignoring the cramps in her legs, she picked her way toward the bank. "It's not as slippery over here. We can move faster." Off to the right, she could still see the trail they had ridden the day of Ryan's accident, but it soon disappeared as the riverbed twisted downward.

Steep dirt banks gave way to rock as the canyon narrowed. Ryan was trotting ahead of her now. She picked up his rhythm, moving forward in a mindless fog. Her limbs felt heavy. She wanted nothing more than to sink into the cool water, rest her back against the bank, and sleep.

Their pounding footsteps echoed, leaving the horrible crackling of flames behind. The water grew deeper as the canyon walls closed in, rushing first above her ankles, then almost to her knees, slowing her down.

She looked up, and a new flash of terror snapped her out of her stupor. Straight in front of them a towering wall of granite blocked the canyon, forcing the water through what looked like a small archway about three feet wide in the rock. She could tell by the way Ryan was running, head down, eyes fixed on the riverbed, that he didn't see it in front of him.

"Ryan, stop!" Her scream bounced like a rock out of a slingshot from one side of the canyon to the other.

Ryan's head snapped up as his feet slipped out from under him. He cried out, then slid toward the gaping archway. Kara dove forward. Her hand connected with the flap on his backpack. The Velcro fastener pulled free, but the nylon held.

She froze, gasping for breath, and stared through the archway where Ryan's legs disappeared. A waterfall! It had to be the same one Ryan was looking at from up on the cliffs the day he fell. Why hadn't she heard its roar? But she knew the reason—the water was too shallow because the weather had been so dry. It wasn't moving fast enough to crash over the edge of the rock with any force.

Kara held on and raised herself slowly to her knees. Her hands still gripped his backpack. Carefully she shifted her hold to his armpits and pulled him back up.

She drew him out of the water toward the side of the canyon just a few feet away. She slipped off his pack, and he wrapped his arms in a death grip around her waist. She held him just as tightly. She could feel his slight body shaking, but the sobs she heard were her own.

She couldn't believe he wasn't hurt. For the second time her brother had almost fallen to his death, and all he had to show for it were cuts and bruises.

"That boy must have a hundred guardian angels." She could almost hear Mom's voice, see her shaking her head. "He's an accident waiting to happen."

"Thank You, God," Kara whispered. It seemed too simple a prayer for what she knew He had done. But she couldn't think of any other words right now.

She sniffed back her tears and looked around. They were trapped. She could see the ledge where Ry had fallen before, high up on the canyon wall. Colin had been right when he said there was a waterfall, but it went through the rocks, not over them. She'd been too worried about Ryan that day to notice.

She wasn't in control of this, not anymore. She dropped her cheek to the top of Ryan's head. They could have died a dozen times today. Like Mom. But they hadn't. That must mean God had a plan. Anne said she needed to learn to trust. Well, she didn't see any way out of this.

"I'm letting go, God. You're the only one who can help us now." She looked up, past the narrow rock walls that shot steeply into the already darkening sky. An eerie, red glow from the fire would soon be their only light.

*Tunnel Falls.* The words stilled her prayer. Anne had talked about this place. "Where the mountains kiss, and the river drops off the edge of the world, there is a door; a pathway to the sky. . . . God knows the way, Little Moon, but only those who truly seek can find it."

Kara closed her eyes. What else had Anne said? Ryan's grip had eased, and he now sagged against her. Her own breathing was so shallow she could barely think. *The rocks. Something about the river racing like wild fire through the mountain.*

*The archway. Tunnel Falls.* "The hidden path!" She nearly shouted it. "We're in the gorge, Ry. The one Anne talked about. We couldn't have come this far if the river was high, but there's hardly any water now."

She couldn't believe it. She had always thought that Anne's story was just folklore, and that there was still only one path out of the valley—the Pine Creek trail. But if this really was Tunnel Falls, and Anne's story was true, then that meant they could get out through here.

She moved him to arm's length and gave him a gentle shake. "Come on, you have to help me; there has to be another way out. It can't be the falls. Look for a cave. A gap in the rocks."

He nodded limply but clung to her leg as she began to run her hands over the rocks and dry brush that covered the canyon walls. As she worked her way toward the falls, Ryan screamed and backed away. She reached for him and tried to pull him close again, but he had wedged himself into a crack in the rock face and refused to budge.

# 25

KARA GRABBED RYAN'S HAND, but he shook his head frantically, shut his eyes, and squeezed farther into the crack.

She took a deep breath and immediately wished she hadn't. The coughing spell almost doubled her over.

"Kara?" She felt his fingers brush her arm. "Kara, you all right?"

His voice broke on a sob. "Don't die, Kara. I'll be good. Please don't die."

She felt like someone had punched her in the stomach. *I'll be good. Don't die.* Just a week ago she'd been feeling guilty that Mom had died. Ryan must be feeling the same. She grabbed him and pulled him with her to sit on the rocky ground. They were both bawling like a couple of babies, and she didn't care.

She held him, rocking back and forth, smoothing his hair, trying to kiss away the hurt like Mom would do. "It's okay, Ry, it's okay."

His body trembled in her arms, and as she held him tighter she felt an overwhelming sense of love.

She'd been so tied up in her own pain, she hadn't realized how much he was hurting too. He was the youngest. He hadn't even been to school before Mom died. Mom was his world. He must miss her as much, or more, than any of them. Kara knew she couldn't let him go on blaming himself. She had to make him understand.

When he finally grew quiet, she forced him to look at her. "It's not your fault, Ryan. Do you hear me? You didn't do anything wrong." She took another deep breath. This time her lungs didn't burn as badly. "I don't know why Mom had to leave us, but she's still alive in heaven. I do know God wants you and me to live down here on earth. Otherwise, we wouldn't be here now.

"Look," she pointed to the break in the cliff where he had been standing. "There's the way out, and you're the one who found it."

"I'm scared," he sobbed.

"That's okay. I am too." She scrambled to her feet and guided his hand to the cliff face where a young tree poked out of a crevice in the rocks. "Hang on to this. I'll go check it out, okay?"

The crack in the rock was just the width of Ryan's shoulders. She bent her head into the opening. Murky light coming from the other end revealed a rough, walled cave. No, it was more like a tunnel than a cave, running straight through the wall of rock.

At the far end of the passageway, she could see nothing but empty sky.

She backed out and studied the area around them more carefully. The river channel acted like a funnel, directing the flow of water, now just a trickle, away from the banks and through the archway in the towering granite wall. Right now this tunnel's floor was dry. If the river ran high, there would be water flowing through here as well, forming a second small waterfall.

She ignored Ryan's whimper as she waded into the water and peered through the archway. Over time, water had eroded the rock. When the water level was higher the river plunged downward, deep into another canyon at the bottom of the falls.

She shivered and moved back toward the tunnel. "I'm going in." The hole was just wide enough for her to squeeze through. The tunnel opened up a little on the inside, but it still wasn't high enough for her to stand upright. She crawled forward. Stretching her hands in front of her, she felt along the walls. Solid rock. Was this the passageway that would lead them out of the gorge?

The tunnel wasn't more than eight feet long. She reached the light and stopped. Hands still pressed against the walls, she leaned forward and peered through. Something bumped her from behind, and she nearly lost her balance.

"What is it, Kara? What's there?"

She sat back on her heels but couldn't turn around. Her heartbeat thudded in her ears. "Ryan Sheridan, don't you ever do that again!"

She could sense him backing away. "Stop. Just hold still, okay? I didn't get a chance to see." She inched forward one more time. Hands braced against the walls, she leaned into the light.

*The edge of the world.* The legend couldn't have been more true. Her stomach flipped, and the floor of the tunnel came up to meet her spinning head. She crouched in the doorway, facing nothingness, and tried to relax her breathing.

*There's a pathway to the sky.* This time she forced her gaze upwards. The cliff face was in shadow. It looked sheer and smooth, but she really couldn't tell. She scanned the side for a rope or vine. If there had ever been one, it was gone.

Ahead of her was only empty space. She squeezed her eyes shut.

"Kara?"

"All right, Ry. Just a minute." She had to think, but she was so tired her brain felt like mush. They had three choices—up, down, or stay put. Up was out for now. The sun had slipped behind the horizon, and from here the light from the fire was only a faint, hazy glow.

Down was unthinkable for the same reason. And also because there was probably nothing there. If they stayed where they were and the fire spread this far, they'd be trapped like a fox in a hole.

End of choices. They'd have to stay and chance it. "Back up, Ry, and let me turn around."

"But I thought you said it was a door. Where does it go?"

"I don't know. It's getting too dark to see." She slid the straps of her backpack off her shoulders. "Take this." A dull ache spread through her back as he pulled the heavy pack away. She heard it drop to the ground.

Her arms scraped against the rough walls, but without the pack she was able to turn completely around. Ryan stood easily in the passage, his shoulders not even touching the sides. Beyond him the patch of gray shadow that was the entrance told her it was already night.

She was still wet, and her skin began to chill under her cotton shirt and jeans. They'd be better off in the tunnel than outside. Ryan was shivering too. "Why can't we go now? I'm hungry."

"We're going to camp here for the night, okay? Let's get into some dry clothes, and then we'll have something to eat."

"Cool." He emptied his pack between them. "I brought jeans and a sweatshirt. Like you said."

"Good. Change your socks too. We'll set our shoes by the opening. Maybe they'll be dry by morning."

While he was changing, she stripped off her own wet clothes. The warmth from her sweatsuit and heavy cotton

147

socks felt like heaven. It was hard to believe only an hour ago she'd been frying in the heat.

They each ate an apple and a pack of raisins, and they shared a bottle of water. When he was done, Ryan dug through his pack and came up with two candy bars. "Want some dessert?"

He was so innocent, so matter-of-fact, she couldn't contain herself. She burst out laughing. "Ryan, you're wonderful." She leaned over and kissed him on the cheek.

"Hey!" He wiped her kiss away with the back of his hand, but even in the murky light she could see his chocolate grin.

The ground inside the tunnel was smooth but hard. Kara spread their heavy jackets end to end, then stretched out on her side with her back against the wall. She used her backpack for a pillow, and Ryan curled into the curve of her body. In less than a minute his even breathing told her he was asleep.

She expected it to be a long night. The tunnel stayed only semidark with the glow of the fire still lighting up the sky. A frail moon peered briefly through the opening to the west, then vanished quickly behind a veil of smoke.

She thought of Colin and Anne. Had they made it out through the Pine Creek trail? "Dear God," she whispered, "they belong to you too. Please keep them safe."

Once she thought she heard the droning of a plane. She rose up on one elbow and listened carefully, but the sound didn't come again. The next time she opened her eyes, both ends of the tunnel were flooded with light.

148

# 26

THIS TIME SHE WAS SURE she heard a plane. She peeled off her socks and squeezed out of the tunnel. The water barely came to her ankles. It was much shallower than last night. Above her, patches of blue sky pushed through the haze. The smoke had cleared some at this end of the valley, but huge, white mushroom clouds still hovered in the north.

She heard the *click, click, whir* of a chopper blade and shielded her eyes to scan the sky. They were too far down, too deep in the canyon. If they couldn't see the helicopter, the helicopter couldn't see them.

Once again she studied the rock face on both sides of the canyon. Too steep. Any ledges were too far up, closer to the top. The granite wall didn't offer a handhold either. At this level, it was worn smooth and slick with moss.

She should go back through the tunnel and explore the other opening, the one on the falls side. Maybe she had missed something last night in the dark. But even the thought made her knees feel weak.

Ryan poked his head out of the tunnel. "What are we going to do, Kara?"

"Maybe we should go back upriver a little ways," she said. At least they could tell where the fire was, and maybe even find a spot to climb out of the canyon. She knew Dad was looking for them. If they could just get to higher ground.

Ryan's brow wrinkled with worry. "What about the fire?"

"We won't go back that far," she promised. "If it gets too hot we'll just turn around. Okay?"

He nodded, then held up his hand. "Shh, listen. It's another plane. Dad's coming for us!"

"He'll find us, Ry, but you have to remember there are other planes too. Dropping chemicals and water on the fire." She tried a smile. "Don't worry, we'll be back home in Lariat by dinnertime."

*Please God, let me be right.*

They ate the last two apples and drank half a bottle of water. "It's going to be hot today. We should save as much water as we can."

They backtracked for half an hour in the shallow river. A thick layer of ashes made the rocks even more slippery. She tried to stay close to the side, where they could lean on the canyon wall for balance. The gorge had widened, and the uphill slope had lessened the distance to the top, but there was still no way to climb out.

The air grew warmer by the minute. Kara wasn't sure if it was from the sun or the fire. The smoke was getting thicker too. Ryan started coughing, and her throat felt sore again.

"Do you have any candy left?"

"Just these." He pulled a half-filled bag of butterscotch out of his pack.

"Good. Look, it's getting smoky again, but I think the gorge really opens up once we get around that curve. If we don't run into fire, we should be able to climb out."

Ryan soaked his bandanna and tied it around his face. "Okay. I'm ready."

She shivered. He was braver than she was. "Let's go," she said, "but if I say get back, you turn around and run. Got it?"

He nodded and slipped his hand into hers, his blue eyes wide and solemn above his blue-and-white bandanna. *Trust.* She wanted to hug him, but they were wasting time.

She felt the urge to run, like Lily after she'd been cooped up in her stall. She settled for a slow jog, but the uphill slope made it harder than ever to breathe. They rounded the corner, and her feet slipped as she skidded to a stop. She grabbed hold of a large boulder to steady herself and gaped at the pile of rubble blocking their way. "I don't believe it! This must have happened overnight."

"Wow! A beaver dam."

Twenty feet in front of them, a snag of trees and branches jammed tight against the canyon walls. Thicker and higher than any beaver dam, it was much more effective. A trickle of water at the bottom was the only sign of any breach.

"No!" Kara felt her throat tighten, and hot tears formed behind her eyes. *Great. Now what are we going to do?* There was obviously no way around. Going over wasn't such a hot idea either. What if the pile gave way, or their legs got tangled in the brush?

Maybe they could dig a hole big enough to crawl through it. She ran forward and began tearing at the branches, breaking off twigs and pieces of scorched bark. She jerked her hand back from a still-smoldering pine cone. She moved over and tried digging at another spot.

Ryan was right beside her. "Yuck, what's that smell?"

The stench nearly knocked her off her feet. She covered her nose and gagged when she saw the deer embedded in the pile, tongue protruding, dead eyes staring straight at her.

"No! No! No!" She screamed and jumped backwards, almost tripping over Ryan. She turned and ran until she reached the boulder, then bent her knees and let her body sink into the nearly dry riverbed. She yanked off her pack and pressed her back against the rock. Solid and strong, it would hold her upright while she tried to think.

What now? All she wanted to do was close her eyes and sleep. Right there in the middle of an empty riverbed. Let the fire rage. The worst of it was miles away, or they had it almost out by now. Who cared?

Ryan slid down beside her. "That deer's a goner, Kara. It can't hurt you."

One look at the disgust on his face and she burst out laughing. She laughed until her nose ran and the tears spilled down her cheeks, and she still couldn't stop.

Ryan giggled, then scooped up a handful of water and threw it in her face. "Stop it. You're weirding out on me."

He sounded so much like Tia, she almost choked. "Okay, okay. Let me catch my breath." She warded off another handful of water and used the tail of her T-shirt to mop her face. "Well, Kiddo, there's sure no way around that mess. I guess we go back to the door in the tunnel." Part of that legend seemed to fit. She could only hope the rest of it was real.

*God knows the way, Little Moon, but only those who truly seek will find.* Anne would say this was a time to trust.

The way back downhill was easier, and they retraced their steps in half the time. Kara didn't stop to think about what she had to do. She couldn't chicken out of this. She was out of options.

She set her pack next to Ryan and eased into the tunnel. "Stay here. I can't have you bumping me."

"Don't go away."

"I won't. I promise."

She crawled through the narrow passageway, took a deep breath, and leaned out of the opening. Once again the feeling of falling into empty space made her stomach do jumping jacks. She gritted her teeth and forced herself to scan the canyon walls on either side. Nothing, just sheer rock.

*Where the mountains kiss, and the river falls.* The mountains kiss. The only place the mountains really touched was here. And if the river were higher, it would fall through in this spot too. *A pathway to the sky.* She wanted to scream. They were here. The sky was up, but there was no pathway on either side of these cliffs!

The only place she hadn't looked last night was down— it had made her too dizzy. She felt her pulse pounding in her ears. *Take it easy, breathe.* She closed her eyes, held on, and thrust her head and shoulders through the opening.

It was now or never. She opened her eyes.

A pebble fell from above her head and landed with a clunk. Without thinking she followed it down with her eyes. She blinked. *I don't believe this.* She could almost see Anne smile.

The granite shelf was a four-foot drop from where she knelt at the end of the tunnel. It was fairly narrow but still large enough to stand on. She kept her eyes on the ledge and stretched out on her stomach like she'd done when she had rescued Ryan. From this position she could see a gaping hole in the rock face just below her. Was it a cave? Another tunnel?

More likely another dead end. Still, she had to find out. She turned around, told Ryan to stay put, and eased herself over the edge.

The ledge cut deep into the rock face. She would never have seen it if she'd stayed in the tunnel. She ducked under the overhang and followed the pathway, keeping her body pressed against the solid rock. Ten steps took her under the empty waterfall. From there an outcrop of boulders sloped like stair steps to the top of the cliff.

# 27

IT TOOK LOTS OF PRAYER and more than a little persuasion to get Ryan down onto the ledge. But once they made it across the canyon, he scrambled up the makeshift staircase like a bear cub up a tree.

They came out onto a high plateau surrounded by dense forest. Nothing on this side of the falls had burned, but the trees and vegetation were so thick they could only move a few feet in each direction. If the ancient path continued, it had long since been overgrown.

"They'll never find us in this. We need to climb back up there." She pointed to the pile of boulders. To her surprise, Ryan didn't argue. He beat her to the top, plopped down on a large, flat rock, and began rummaging through the contents of his survival bag.

She leaned into the cleft of two gigantic rocks and scanned the valley with her binoculars. Charred and burning trees dotted the smoldering landscape. On this side of the river, the fire had burned almost to the abandoned campsite where they had tied their horses the day Ryan fell off the cliff. It seemed like a year ago instead of just a week.

"It's still burning. I can see some flames, but it looks like they've got it contained." She was glad she couldn't see Eagle

Lodge from here. If it was ashes, she didn't want to know about it. At least not right now. She couldn't see Otter Lake either, but from the looks of the smoke, the fire could easily have burned that far.

Kara heard the drone of another plane. She caught a flash of light from its wing, then lost it behind a veil of smoke. "They're dumping water, not looking for us. We need to do something to attract their attention."

"We could signal with a mirror. Colin said that's what you do when you're lost in the woods."

"That's great, Ry, but I haven't got a mirror. Dad had all of the survival gear packed away with his hunting stuff. I didn't have time to find it."

"I have this. Here." He handed her a small, round piece of glass that had been polished to a sheen.

"Where'd you get this?"

"I found it at that camp. Where I found my bullets. Isn't it cool? All you got to do is flash it in the sun. Dad will see it and come and get us."

She laughed. "It's worth a try. I don't know about you, but I'm ready to get out of here."

It was easy to catch a beam of sunlight in the glass. She reflected it off the trees, then the rocks, and finally into the sky. After twenty minutes, she was ready to scream. "It's no good. They're too far away."

She sat down beside him on the rock. "You wouldn't have a steak in there, would you? I'm so hungry I could eat a bear."

She got the smile she'd been looking for. "Nope. But we can eat more raisins." He handed her a package, then opened one for himself.

"What else do you have in there?"

"Just my bullets. I shined them up real good." He poured the handful of empty cartridges onto the rock. Two books of matches slipped out of the canvas bag.

"Ryan Sheridan!" She shook her head. How could she scold him? Matches were one of the most important requirements for a survival kit. So far his treasures had really come in handy.

And so would these. "Fire! That's the answer. Ryan, take your bag and go get me some dry twigs, pine needles, moss—anything we can use for kindling."

His eyes got wide. "You're gonna start another fire?"

"Don't worry, we'll keep it small, right here on these rocks. That's what they're looking for, Ry. The smoke will get them over here fast."

"All right! Smoke signals." He scrambled off the rock.

Kara pocketed the matches, then pushed aside the rest of Ryan's things to make space for the fire. She swept the empty cartridges into a pile. They would help to shield the first tiny spark, and they would reflect the heat back into the fire.

"Here, Kara, I brought lots. And some bigger pieces too."

She crumbled some dried moss into a pile, then added pine needles and stacked twigs tepee style around the pile. "Kneel here, Ry. Shield it from the breeze." The dry tinder caught on the first try. She blew on it until the twigs were burning well, then added some rotting tree bark and crossed a couple small pieces of deadwood over the top.

"Soak your bandanna and squeeze it out, and we'll use it like a blanket to trap the smoke."

They each gripped two corners of the bandanna and held it over the fire, just out of reach of the flames. When the trapped smoke had built up, they lifted the cloth away, sending puffs of cloud-white smoke high into the air.

Ryan coughed and had to step away. "Careful, Ry. Try not to breathe it. We might have to do this a while."

"No we won't. Listen."

There was no mistaking the sound of an airplane engine as it swooped by overhead. And no mistaking the familiar brown-and-green logo as the plane circled lower for another pass.

"Dad!" Ryan was jumping up and down, waving his arms, yelling at the top of his lungs. "He sees us! He sees us!"

The third circle was as low as she'd ever seen Dad fly. She raised her hands above her head. Two thumbs up. She sent the message, "We're all right."

Dad signaled a thumbs up back, then flew off.

"He's leaving us here!" Ryan cried. "Why, Kara?"

"It's okay, Ry," she assured him. "Dad can't land the plane in here. He's going back to send help. We need to wait right here—they'll come get us."

If there was any sweeter music than the clatter of chopper blades, it had to be the forest ranger's voice as he pushed through the brush to meet them. "You kids okay?"

Thirty minutes later they set down at the airport in Lariat. Dad was waiting on the tarmac. He lifted Ryan from the chopper, and Kara saw the dark circles around his eyes. She knew he hadn't slept, but she was shocked to see the stubble on his cheeks and chin was mostly gray. He hugged them both so tightly she thought her ribs would crack.

In the pilots' lounge, she accepted the cup of coffee Mark handed her, then groaned when he offered her an apple. "Forget the apple. I want french fries and a hamburger."

He grinned back at her. "You're on. But I'm afraid it'll have to wait. I think your dad wants to take you home."

Dad was already bundling Ryan into the car. She bit her lip. "Colin and Anne were up at Otter Lake. The chopper pilot said there's been no sign of them."

Mark stared at her, then shook his head. "I was just up there. That area's still burning itself out."

Dad walked toward the open office door. "Come on, Sugar Bear, let's get you home."

157

"I can't, Dad. Colin and Anne are still out there." She looked up at his tired face. *Please, please understand.* "They would have taken the Pine Creek trail. I have to help look for them."

She expected him to order her to the car. Instead, his shoulders sagged, and she saw the resignation in his eyes. "I had a feeling you'd say something like that." He rubbed at the stubble on his chin. "Look, let me get Ryan home. I'll get someone to stay with him, then we'll have Sheriff Lassen put a posse together."

She shook her head. Now that Ryan was safe, all she could think about was Colin and Anne. "That will take too much time. We need to go now. Who knows what could have happened to them."

"You stay with Ryan, Dad. I'll go," said her older brother.

She hadn't heard Greg come in, but now he stood just behind Dad in the doorway. He looked like he'd been rolling in ashes, except for the rashlike blisters covering his hands and face. "You okay, Sis?"

She nodded. "You look like you had a fight with a grizzly and lost."

His teeth grinned white behind the soot. "The grizzly may have won, but the fire didn't." He looked at Dad. "It missed the lodge. We lost one cabin, and it looks like something caved in the barn, but the main buildings are fine."

"Thank God!" She didn't realize she'd said it out loud until she saw the surprise on Greg's face.

"Yeah." He rubbed his forehead against the sleeve of his jumpsuit. "Let me get out of this tux. Then we'll load some horses in the trailer and get up there. From the looks of it a while ago, the upper part of the trail was passable."

# 28

KARA DIDN'T KNOW WHAT had happened, but in the few days since she had seen him last, Greg had really changed. She sat in the cab of the truck between him and Bud Davis. Greg was quiet but polite. And he looked different. Resigned. That was the word. The anger that had plagued him since Mom had died was gone.

*He's accepted Mom's death.* With a feeling of shock, she realized that she had too.

Mr. Davis squeezed her arm. "Don't you worry, Honey. God's gonna get them two found. You just bet on it."

They were getting closer. The horses in the big slant-load trailer started stomping around. "Hey, what's going on back there?"

Kara bent the mirror so she could see into the open window at the front of the trailer. "They smell something. Maybe the smoke's got them spooked."

Greg shook his head. "Not these guys. They've been on fire cleanup crews. That's why I brought them."

"There's your answer." Bud nodded to the open meadow. It spread three acres wide from the dirt road to the trailhead. Two horses stood smack in the middle, munching on the sparse, green grass.

159

"Lily and Dakota!" Kara didn't know whether to laugh or cry. "No saddles or tack. That must mean Colin or Anne took it off. Which means they must be alive."

She saw the set of Greg's chin and knew what he was thinking. Colin and Anne could have released the horses—turned them loose so they'd at least have a chance to escape.

When Kara jumped out of the truck, Lily nickered and trotted over. She rubbed her muzzle against Kara's shoulder. Dakota came willingly too. Kara let Greg check Dakota out while she ran her hands all over Lily's body, down her legs, even checking inside her mouth for sores.

"She's got a few scorch marks, but she's sound." Kara felt the tightness building in her chest and pressed her face against Lily's side. *Not now. You don't have time to cry.*

"Dakota's got a cut above his fetlock," Greg said. "It doesn't look like anything serious, and he's not lame. I say we take him in. He might be able to lead us to Colin." He glanced at Bud. "Besides, he's strong. He can carry two if he has to."

Bud nodded. "We'll ride him and pony one of the others."

Kara patted Lily's flank, then followed Mr. Davis back to the trailer. "I'll get some gear for Lily too. I'd rather ride her than one of the others."

When the horses were ready, Kara gripped Lily's mane, grabbed the saddle horn, and vaulted into the saddle. "Let's go. Anne and Colin are down there somewhere, or these two wouldn't have stuck around."

Bud Davis frowned. "I don't know. We're supposed to wait for Sheriff Lassen and his men."

*In your dreams.*

Greg laughed. "When my sister gets that look in her eye, you might as well give up the fight."

Lily danced along the trail, settling only when the path got too steep to do anything but slide. She needed to run.

Kara kept a tight rein and patted the mare's neck. "Easy girl. We'll get some exercise later. Right now we have work to do."

The trail zigzagged for a hundred yards along a narrow ridge, then settled into easy curves for half a mile. Kara eased her grip on Lily's reins and looked around for any fresh tracks in the dirt and rocks. She grimaced as the familiar acrid smell stung her nostrils.

The fire had not reached this part of the mountain, but as they rounded a curve, she saw smoke smothering the tree tops like a thick, gray quilt. She couldn't see the bottom of the trail, but she knew it snaked with hairpin turns down into the murk.

Greg brought Dakota alongside Lily. "We won't get far in that."

"Let's hope we don't have to." She tried not to show her real thoughts. She wasn't giving up that easily. If she had to, she'd go on her own.

She clicked her tongue. Lily obeyed the command and moved forward, then once again tried to break into a trot. Kara held her in check until suddenly the mare put on the brakes, and nothing Kara did could make her budge.

Dakota whinnied, coming up on Lily's tail. Both horses jigged in place. "Back him off!" she yelled at Greg.

"I'm trying."

Lily spun around on the narrow trail, and for one terrifying moment Kara thought they would both go over the side.

Bud's horse stood calmly a few paces behind Greg and Dakota.

Bud held his hand up for silence. "Shh. Listen."

Even the horses quieted, but both Lily's and Dakota's ears were twitching like radar. A low whistle, weak and thin, sent them dancing once more.

161

"It's them," Kara whispered, "it's got to be." She jumped out of the saddle and began searching the brush. Greg was right beside her when she saw a pair of boots sticking out of a rock. As she slid down the rocky slope, she was glad to be wearing her heavy jeans.

Colin was propped in a sitting position, half in and half out of what looked to be a small cave. He grinned at her. "Hi there, Indian Princess. I see you brought the cavalry."

Before she could think of anything to say, he closed his eyes.

Greg pushed past her and pressed two fingers against Colin's neck, then lifted one eyelid. "He's alive, just out cold."

"Wakara?" The whispered question came from inside the cave.

"Anne! He found her. Colin found Anne. She must be hurt, or she would have come out." Her pulse throbbing wildly, she pushed past Greg and Colin and rushed into the cave.

▲

All they had to go on was Colin's story. Anne couldn't remember anything after lightning struck a nearby tree and sent her rolling down an embankment into Otter Lake. He had found her lying partially in the water, one leg twisted up and under her at an impossible angle.

"She was so white I thought she was dead. But she screamed like a wildcat when I tried to move her." He grinned at Anne, who lay in a hospital bed, her right leg swathed from toes to hip in a hard plaster cast.

She glared at him, but Kara could see the spark of humor in her dark eyes. "You would not make the best nurse, I think. Better you stick with horses."

"Hey, the doc said I did a good job setting that leg."

Everyone laughed, and Dad shook his head. "Tree bark and fishing line. What's that old saying? 'Necessity is the mother of invention.'"

Colin doubled over with a coughing spell.

"I'll get some water." Kara grabbed a paper cup and filled it at the small sink, then waited until he caught his breath.

"I think we've stayed long enough," Dad intervened. "Kara starts school tomorrow and Colin needs to get home. He's not even supposed to be out of bed yet."

Kara heartily agreed. Colin had already described their ordeal to the doctors, to Sheriff Lassen, and then to the rest of them. She shuddered every time she thought about it.

She could almost feel the heat of the flames closing in, the embers catching Colin's shirt on fire. He had rolled in the lake, then soaked Dakota's saddle blanket, wrapped it around Anne, and laid her in front of him across the horse's back.

"I have to tell you I was scared," Colin had said. "Dakota wanted out of there bad, and I couldn't see two feet in front of me. He took off, and I figured we were headed in the right direction when we ran into Lily.

"Her reins had snagged a tree limb. It slowed her down, but it sure didn't stop her. When I cut her loose, she took off like an arrow straight up the side of the mountain. That's when I knew we'd found the Pine Creek trail."

He had swallowed enough smoke to make him dizzy and had fallen off Dakota twice. The second time, Anne slid off with him, and he knew he couldn't get her back on. He had cracked three ribs. "But I didn't even feel it then. I just knew we had to head for cover."

He had taken the saddles and bridles off the horses, turned them loose, and dragged Anne down the slope into the shallow cave. "I figured if the fire hit us we were goners.

If not, someone would be along sooner or later to get us out of there."

Kara felt tears well up in her eyes. She turned away and tossed the empty paper cup in the trash can. Every time she thought about how close Colin and Anne had come to death, she lost it. She had come to realize just how much they both meant to her—Colin maybe more than she wanted to admit.

Greg and Ryan pushed past her on their way out the door. "See ya at home."

Bud Davis slapped his hat on his head and shook Dad's hand. "I think I'll head on out too, Harley. You just let me know if there's anything more I can do."

Kara caught the look the men exchanged and realized her suspicions had been right. Mr. Davis had been shepherding Greg.

Dad's words confirmed her thoughts. "I can't thank you enough, Bud. Lord willing, we won't be needing you for a while."

Mr. Davis squeezed her shoulder as he left. "You have a fine family here, Wakara. You take care now."

Dad was helping Colin to his feet. "Okay, okay, I'm ready," Colin was saying.

He grinned at Kara, then straightened and looked at her dad, his face more serious than she had ever seen it.

"I've got exactly two weeks to get well. The youth group at church is busing it to Bend for the football game. Thought I'd tag along and keep Wakara company," he said quietly. "If that's okay with you."

# 29

Tia squealed. "Just like that?"

"Shh!" Kara nodded, laughing. "Yeah. Colin said it just like that. You should have seen the look on Dad's face. I thought he was going to say no. Then he smiles and says, 'Well, son, it's fine with me, but you'd better clear it with the boss.'

"At first I thought he meant Anne, but he was looking right at me. I was so embarrassed I could have died."

"Whoo," Tia shouted, "I am totally impressed. I can't believe you didn't tell me before!"

"When? Between Colin and Anne, we've been at the hospital every day, then I had to get Ryan ready to start school. I haven't seen you long enough to say hi, let alone tell you about a football game."

Tia threw her an exasperated look. "Whatever." She whirled around and walked backwards. "Whooee, wait 'til Amber and Heather find out."

Kara snagged an apple from the tree at the end of the driveway and snapped the stem off with her teeth. "Find out what? It's not like we're going on a real date. Besides, Mr. and Mrs. Andrews will be along."

Tia groaned and picked an apple for herself. "Mr. and Mrs. Eagle Eye."

Kara laughed. "It's okay. Colin won't be able to do much more than sit and cheer. His ribs are still taped."

It was only the second week in September, but already the weather had changed. The trees were turning color and Kara's boots crunched over a few red-amber leaves scattered across the gravel road from the bus stop to the ranch.

"Look." She pointed to a trail of smoke that spiraled upward from the chimney. "Anne must be here. Dad sent Colin after her this morning before he took off for the lodge."

After her short stay in the hospital, Dad announced Anne was coming to the ranch to stay.

"We need her, Sugar Bear. This way you can concentrate on school, and Ryan can have someone here when he gets home."

Kara had to admit she was glad. It would be nice to not always have to be the one in charge.

Dad and Greg had been back and forth from Lariat to Eagle Lodge several times since the fire. Dad had said this morning that they were almost finished with the repairs. Well, except for the barn, which, according to Colin, would take a six-man crew and a hunk of money to restore. Dad wasn't sure it was worth it.

Kara stopped to take off her boots, and Tia beat her to the kitchen. Anne was sitting at the white oak table peeling apples. Her bare toes were sticking out of the walking cast she had propped on a chair.

Tia's eyes lit up. "Pie?"

"Applesauce. Wash your hands, please. First cocoa, then you help."

Kara washed, then went to the stove and poured the hot chocolate into heavy ceramic mugs. She set a cup in front

166

of Anne. "Are you sure you should be doing this? Tia and I could handle it."

"I am fine. It is time I go back to work."

It was strange to see Anne in their kitchen using Mom's best paring knife. A month ago Kara would have resented it, accused her of trying to take Mom's place.

Tia was digging through a cardboard box on the other end of the table. "Hey, looks like your dad brought back some of your stuff."

Anne nodded. "He brought Ryan's things too. You will need to clean them. Everything will do except some of the clothes."

Kara groaned. Anne was right. Her denim skirt and white silk blouse looked like they'd been rolled in the fireplace.

Tia held up a red cotton shirt and a pair of cutoffs. "Hey, there's nothing wrong with these." She grinned and wrinkled her nose, "If you don't mind smelling like Smokey the Bear."

They sorted the clothes into piles—one for the trash bin and one for the washing machine. Then Kara lifted two chunks of newspaper from the bottom of the box.

She unwrapped the smallest first. Her mother's face smiled at her out of the tarnished silver frame. Tia turned away, and Anne's head bent over the growing pile of apple skins.

*Oh, Mom, I miss you so much. We've had a pretty rough year.* She grabbed a cloth from the linen drawer and dug some silver polish out of the cleaning closet.

Tia opened the other package. "Hey, cool. Your great-grandfather's drawing. It's fine, see? Not even a smudge." She looked from the portrait to Kara, then Anne. "I don't know. If your great-grandmother was Nez Perce, she sure doesn't look like Anne. Neither do you. Maybe she was from the Yana people."

167

Kara took the picture and set it on the counter next to her mother's. She tried to imagine her ancestor with short, curly hair and green-blue eyes. Impossible.

"Does it still bother you?" Anne's quiet question startled her.

"I don't think so. At least not as much. But I'd still like to find out for sure someday."

To tell the truth, she hadn't thought about it since before the fire. Was the first Wakara Nez Perce like Great-grandfather had thought, or Yana, which would explain her name? Somehow it didn't matter as much as it used to.

"She's the same person either way. And so am I. But I'm still going to read your father's book. I'd really like to know more about the Yana people."

Anne only nodded, but Wakara was sure she saw a gleam of approval behind her smile.

**Linda Shands** is a prolific writer of magazine articles and the author of four adult novels and one nonfiction book. She loves the Oregon wilderness and lives in the small town of Cottage Grove with her husband, a cat, two horses, and twin golden retrievers.

# Blind Fury

Wakara learns more about being a child of God but struggles to trust Him. When her dad and brother get lost in a snowstorm, Wakara has to think fast and pray hard to try to save them—and herself.

0-8007-5747-5

Coming Fall 2001. . .

# White Water

Wakara, Tia, Ryan, and Colin fall overboard during a rafting trip. Ryan is swept downstream and Wakara insists on going after him, in spite of all the dangers. When a black bear attacks, will Wakara lose another person she loves?

0-8007-5772-6